She Belongs To The Game

The Game

Part 1. A Pimp's Sister

By Tamba Beasley

This book is dedicated to Oakland Ca. Where it is apart of our culture to either be a Pimp or a Hoe. Where this lifestyle is detrimental to our mental health and struggling upbringings. This book is for every teenage girl who has been exposed without permission or the knowledge to even choose. Your either a hoe or a pimp in life, and that choice is yours.

"The Game is still to be sold, if ever told."

Tamba

CONTENTS

Prologue

"What would you say is the general issue?" There was a therapist asking D.J a million questions. He got tricked into a session related to his mental health. Unaware of any issues that he was currently facing, of course D.J was pissed. The entire session was full of rage, and drama, and who gets the blame. He blamed his mother and continuously said "She left me." The therapist sat there silent because she could feel his pain. The heartache of an abandoned child was burning through her professional years of experience. You can't learn this in school, because shit like this cuts you deep in real life. "I'm not a bad kid, I have goals to you know?" D.J broke the silence.

"Tell me some of your goals, I'd like to hear them." She smiled at D.J hoping it would give him a sense of trust. "First, I promise to get Sydni, nobody can have her! Nobody." "Ok why don't you tell me more, is Sydni your sister?" the therapist asked. "Yes she's my little sister and I plan to get her from the system one day. I swear I'll have more money than you, than every fucking body in this weak ass building." He was broken and the notes from the session reflected several mental disorders, but was it just trauma? Or could it be hurt turned into ambition? That's how a goal works anyway, right? When you want something you go crazy, meaning you give it all you got until you achieve it.

Chapter 1

A Rough Start

I remember my mom as well as a child could remember having ice cream after dinner, that lady was something else, loved her with everything within me but I never did understand her. In Jan 1987 she gave birth to my older brother Daniel Jr. and about seven years later, in Dec. 1994, me, Sydni. We didn't have much of nothing growing up, but she made the best out of what we had. I knew we were blessed when I started to understand how much the shelters and the community churches helped us out weekly. My mom would also get a welfare assistance check, so in a way, we never went without. The shelter gave us clothes, canned goods, and a little bit more than most churches. Sometimes the mothers of the church would make dinners for us to take home. The assistance though, it made my mom feel like she was good, so naturally her children felt the same. I grew out of that feeling quickly, but I watched my mom as she remained content with this life. Even though she had a side hustle, I didn't believe she was doing that for us. I think it really just became a social habit, something she did for her own pleasure, a lifestyle I'mage. The day my mother met my father was also the day she made a commitment to him and decided to become a part of his team. I don't know too much about her life before me, and I can't tell you much about my pops either, but the streets have told me for years. I've heard all kinds of stories about my mother. They say she was already dealing with a P (pimp) when she actually decided to choose up on my dad, and this created a big problem. They say this dude was controlling and that my mom could never really shake him. "Melody! Mel" that's my mom's name, though some people called her "Passion". The first time I heard that name I wasn't sure if the guy had said it to my mom by mistake or what but I remember it very well.

One day, the neighbor was politely yelling my mom's name "Ms. Melody, Melody..." as she stumbled into the hallway of our apartment complex. "What the fuck is it, Linda? Let me be. I'm going inside to my kids," my mom said. I was playing right outside the door as she passed without even noticing me. "This is the third time this week that you've been a disturbance to this community. I'll have to report you Monday morning!" Ms. Linda was pretty nice to my mom and would even come by to check on my brother and I whenever we were left home alone. I never felt like she was out to get us, I mean my mom was butt ass naked in the middle of the day. Linda tried and tried but after so many warnings, she had to report my mom and this time it was pretty bad. Plus, my mom had knots on her head, and let's not forget, she was naked. Her ass was pretty well portioned, and she had a very tiny waist, so it indeed was a disturbance.

Moms was sexy as hell, I promise you. Her body and facial appearance was great, and she definitely was comfortable with herself. So I wasn't surprised to find out my mom had already been standing naked outside maybe a full hour for the world to see. She was having an altercation with her pimp who had snatched one of her thin ass dresses off of her in the heat of an argument.

"Did you just snatch my mutha fucking dress?" She said to her pimp "Bitch shut up and get in the car. Here, here's your thin ass dress, let's go NOW!" He replied. That's when my mom said "No! I'm done" They started to argue going back and forth until she made a break for it and tried to run. The nigga snatched my mom by her arm quickly and began to pound on her face. He wore jewelry, rings on every finger, so with each hit a knot surfaced. My mom was a good actress though, she dropped to the ground pretending to be faint. "Aye, bitch get yo ass up and let's go." He yelled as he walked around to the driver seat of his car. Within seconds, she jumped up and started to run home. The dude followed her and kicked in the downstairs door of the apartment complex. He caught Mel and dragged her ass back down from the top stair. "What the fuck nigga, just let me leave!" She cried out "bitch it don't work like that." He smacked her up some more then carried her this time, and put her ass in the car. Dude made it half way up the block before moms woke up and hopped out the car in the middle of an intersection on high street and Mac. I was told that my mom was trying to leave the guy for the millionth time, and that's when she ran home naked and all beaten up. "Linda, I don't care. Do what you have to do, I ain't harm no one. In fact, someone harming me. Shit, I should be the one calling for help." Mel was so drunk and I could barely make out her words. "You continue to deal with this guy who's broken lights and doors on this property, putting other tenants in danger; I won't allow it anymore! And my goddamn name is Karen...not Linda" My mom had called this lady Linda for the few years we lived there, so naturally I did the same and called the lady Linda. She was pissed off, and slammed her door shut, leaving my mom to fumble with her own house keys.

That's when the guy came quietly up the stairs and stood behind her. I watched as her hands shook at the thought of him coming, and when he leaned closer, breathing in her ear, I could see that she had then realized she moved too damn slow. "Passion!" he whispered... It was him; I could finally put a face to this man to whom she would tense up during phone calls. My life began to make sense. He was the reason she'd squeeze my hand tight when we got to 20th and E.14th.

Mel would always say, "We're almost there baby, let's run a little." So, we'd run and skip and sing until we made it to the park between 16th and 18th Ave. on Foothill Blvd. That's where she would let me play, and I'd see her from a distance smiling with a Mexican or an Asian man. The whole time, our park date was her actually busting a damn date.

Now look at her standing at our front door, stuck. I watched this man fill up with aggression, and release it by giving my mom a nibble on her ear. It was scary to watch as he began to turn her to face him. She was breathing hard. He squeezed her ass and thighs, and that's when he told her "I'll always love you baby, you my Passion."

At five years old I could see that this man loved her, but not in the right way. He was so aggressive with her, like an addict. Had he fallen in love with the idea of my mom changing his life? I wonder why he wasn't ok with her changing her own. Some nights, this same dude would come by when I was asleep, but my brother "D.J" would be woke and hear him say to our mom, "'Baby, you gone take us to the next level." That was his focus through rain, summer, and snow — to reach the next level. I heard people say my mom was more like a renegade anyway, and would use him for her convenience. So instead of taking them to the next level, she played game after game. Mel would never give up her full trap, or any full amount of money she made to any of her supposed pimps. I don't get why she was even a prostitute in the first place. Where was her mom, dad, family or any friends to encourage her? No one thought to tell her she was better? No one could tell her or encourage her because she'd cut ties with everybody, and eventually lost her way.

My dad was a better man. I mean, of course, he intended to pimp her also, but eventually he wanted her out of the game. Sure, he knocked her and introduced her to another part of the lifestyle, but he really was a better man to her. He only treated my mom according to the way she carried and treated herself. That all changed one day when he got her pregnant with their first child, a boy, his Jr. My dad was happy, and everyone always said they believed he would do right by Mel. For as long as he could, that's exactly what he did. He took care of her and my big brother Daniel Jr. but Mel couldn't leave the life behind her.

"I'm taking my son, if you don't stop busting dates!" Daniel Jr aka "DJ" was barely two, and mom was back at it curb side, ten toes down, day in and day out leaving Jr. with just any and everybody. Those relapses in her life would be times when she would run into C.J. That's the insecure controlling pimp. He was the main reason my pops didn't want her out there. Pops would see her and suggest that she go home. "What's up my love? I'ma ask you again to get the fuck off the curb and focus on our son." "No D! I'm cool off that, I'm trynna make this money, for us babe." "Mel, you my baby mom. I don't need you selling pussy for us. I got us." My dad tried to convince her, but she wasn't having it.

What more could he do? This is why you're not supposed to have kids with your hoe in the first place. Pops just wanted to do right by his children, but my mom was super hardheaded and wouldn't listen to nothing. That same day, she saw C.J slide through the blade where she was at, and he claimed Mel owed him a large amount of money. "Aye Passion, you can't post out here until you pay me what you owe me." He rolled his window down to make sure she saw he meant business but Mel couldn't give a fuck and replied, "I don't owe you shit C.J, we closed that chapter. I'm D's bitch now and that's my daddy, that's who I answer to." C.J exploded. "Bitch, none of that don't matter until you pay me, you still my bitch and I'll beat your ass still." He stepped out his car and slapped my mom hard to the ground. "C, hold up it's me your baby remember, please stop" she begged him. "Don't make me embarrass you bitch! This shit ain't a game," he replied. See this that shit right here! My mom was playing with this man and consequences come to a bitch trying to make her own rules. Quickly word got back to my dad, so naturally he wanted to protect Mel, but pops was so young that he wasn't even sure if he was giving his family his best and after hearing all of what had happened that day he began to feel torn about saving a bitch, despite who the bitch was.

My aunt was watching Jr. when pops busted through the front door pissed. He had driven all around town looking for Mel, so now all he could do was wait until she showed up. A few hours went by and my mom finally came creeping in slowly. "Mel where the fuck you been, I looked for you, why didn't you call me?" My dad had a million questions. "I can handle it D." She then pretended to feel bad and claimed to stop hoeing that same day. It was pathetic, same never ending story until she actually stopped, I mean really tried this time. That just made my dad step all the way up and in. He continued to pimp and run his program but he also had a family now, so he had to balance the two.

My pops had a different style of pimping; his just came naturally. My brother would always tell me these childhood stories of our dad because I can't recall ever meeting him. I guess Mel held back from the streets as long as she could but the moment that she dropped me into this world, she didn't sit around to heal, she just hit the streets, curbside 10 toes down. Just like that, she was back in the game. Mel didn't let one kid stop her, so Imagine what number two did. She just used us as an excuse to get out the house and get some air. "I'm young Daddy, I don't want this life let me go please." She enjoyed being a night worker living free with no rules, but she kept running into her old pimp C.J. and that should have been her sign. "Caught up to you again huh bitch?" "I'm just passing through I'm not working C." "Naw we got unfinished business," he said, and this time, he opened up the back of his van and snatched her ass up.

Mel was with C.J for a few days before my pops found her and they were beefing ever since. This dude would sweat my mom for years and my dad's friends started to get disrespectful with him saying stuff like, "my nigga we beefing over a bitch." They wasn't taking his street cred serious any longer. "She not just a bitch my nigga, this my baby momma and my kids need her."

The type of man my dad presented himself to be was rare. He kept calm but stood his ground and didn't care what anyone had to say about him. His only focus was his kids, and he knew he had to move us before things got out of control. One day he woke up on that hype and told my mom, "We moving; ASAP." Surprisingly, she listened to his plans, but Mel had other plans. My mom was a hustler first before anything and sometimes I wondered, damn did she even love us? Love us enough to stop? Did I think she was good at hustling? Hell no! She didn't follow the rules, she would just wing her way out of shit and every day felt like a new day for her to try again. No one's perfect but how many days of trying before you wake up to build something, to make it happen now? Honestly, my mom messed up big time and it left D.J and I scarred for life.

I was six years old when they found her body, she took two bullets to the head. What a life, huh? D.J knew our pops very well, but me, not so much. When I was three, he pretty much gave up fighting with my mom and left for good. I rarely saw him in person, but we did have many phone conversations and I had lots of pictures of him as well.

My mom never moved, my Pops kept progressing and moved to Atlanta. He was back and forth out of state to tend to us, but he grew tired of my mom. The visit grew shorter and shorter, eventually he would just send us everything we needed. My brother hated it, but he blamed mom, and even I was starting to think it really was her fault. "Mom, why can't we just listen to dad and move?" I remember we were eating dinner one day when D.J asked my mom about us moving, she never wanted to talk about shit but this time she started spazzing.

"I don't know why he left, I don't know what to do since he left, I don't know, I'm confused with myself." Tears ran down her face. "Mommy, mommy why are you crying? It's ok mommy." I leaned on the table trying to wipe my mom's tears. "Mom, you ok?" D.J asked her, but she didn't reply quick enough and that's when he jumped up, flipping the chair backwards from moving so fast and decided to tell our mom about herself.

"You just a weak ass bitch! Two kids you don't even know what to do with us, chasing a nigga, Sydni will never be like you!" I knew he loved me more than she ever could. Imagine how scary it was to know your life was in an adult's hands but that adult was not capable of providing, let alone parenting children. I watched my brother transition, that day, he felt hopeless. I knew he wasn't going to let our life play out that way, he was determined to be better and that's when he started bag chasing at the age of 12.

Would you believe my mom continued on and went out that night like usual? Only this time, she went missing the entire week and when they found her, she was dead. A witness said she was arguing with one man when another arrived to pick her up and the first man put two bullets in her head quickly after he was also pronounced dead and the second guy fled the scene.

The story headlined all over the news because they were looking for the second John Doe. I remember everyone around me reading the newspaper that week. I remember crying for my mom, then attending her funeral, she never came back, she never called to say goodbye she just went to live in heaven. It was downhill from there. It was a battle within my mom's family who were getting custody of my brother and I, but none of them being stable enough to provide for us either, it was a disaster, honestly.

"Wake up Sydni we're leaving." Daniel woke me out of my sleep one evening he was whispering and shhh's-ing me like we're running away. "D.J, are we running away?" I asked. "Yea we gotta get outta here, these people gone have us jacked up in the head." My brother was smart, but he was also just a kid and I mean, how far did he think he would actually get us? From there we were back and forth between relatives when they finally gave my aunt full custody of us both. "I got y'all now nephew, auntie gon do right by you both I promise." Well she made a fucking promise she couldn't keep. We figured she just couldn't take the thought of raising us alone and got hooked on drugs, the easiest thing to do. My momma wasn't even on drugs. Yea she would come home drunk and pass out but high off of drugs was something new. My auntie wasn't mentally stable; she was all messed up in the head and the drugs were her only outlet. It was embarrassing honestly, and I hated running into her on the bus.

D.J would say, "Dang Sid, there goes auntie Tanya, just look away act like you don't see her." We would pretend we couldn't see her, and she'd come stumbling over to us. "Nephew I'ma be home to cook you and Sydni dinner tonight; let me just get two dollars I'll be there, I promise."

D.J would get so mad. "What I look like catering to you, get out my face with them lies lady you ain't coming home and you ain't cooking us dinner." She'd given us another broken promise and this was our guardian for a year straight. It was a routine for us, paying the rent, making dinner, all of the things you needed an adult for as a kid. My auntie wouldn't come home most nights and we actually liked it that way because whenever she did come, we would walk in on her shooting up in the bathroom or even worse, she'd wake us up asking for money to get more drugs. What disturbed me most was the smell of burning crack out of her dirty old pipe. We would threaten to kick her out and that's when she would snap out of crack head mode. "Y'all some damn kids; y'all can't kick me out and this my house anyway!" We had enough of her but eventually auntie Tanya died of a drug overdose, and as much as we didn't want to be around her, it hurt us bad.

One morning D.J found her passed out foaming from the mouth with the band tied tight around her arm. He said her veins were bulging, ready to burst. Family and friends came day to day as we prepared for the funeral.

The day came and I couldn't believe how she'd fought so hard to get us just to let us go. I shook my head during the viewing and from behind me you could hear a person angry. 'Stupid just stupid. How could you let us down? I knew we couldn't depend on you! I can't depend on no bitch." D.J stood over her lifeless body crying and mumbling those words as he slammed her casket shut. The funeral filled with whispers. "Why would he do that, it's her funeral?" one person whispered, but D.J didn't care anymore, we loved our auntie but hated what she had become.

Now everybody would see D.J filled with anger as he became numb, heartless. Shit started happening so fast, one minute I was changing out of my black dress, the next minute I was lost in the system. Daniel was lucky his teacher took him in, she had a strong grip on him and wasn't letting D.J go out like that, On the other hand things were different for me. I was younger and our social worker felt I needed a family of my own to grow up with and move past all our tragedies. When another year went by, my brother started to trip out on everyone. They had moved me around from placement to placement but there was nothing steady for me. It got really sickening. I was eight and suicidal, until one day he came, my big brother came and rescued me.

Daniel's teacher was helping him move forward with emancipation and in the meantime, he'd convinced her to fully adopt me. "Wow it worked!" I said jumping in my brother's arms as we left the social worker's office. I was in disbelief. My brother really kept his word, and on each visit he would say, "I'm not gon leave you Sid, I promise." As bad as I wanted to believe him, I prepared for the worst, but he was standing in my face grinning hard all proud and shit. "What you ain't think a nigga was gon come back for his little sister?" I don't even think he really realized what he had accomplished. He knew somebody had to step up, he had to be our dad. D.J brought me home that evening to Ms. Lauren's house, weird as this may sound but bro was fucking his teacher. I already knew it just because I knew my brother, so of course the moment I walked in the door, she greeted me with open arms and made me feel more at home than I'd ever felt in my life. "You made us dinner?" My mouth dropped. I wasn't used to this type of shit. It was corn, dinner rolls with melted butter on top, some meat loaf and asparagus with stuffed mashed potatoes and all types of drinks in the fridge and she even had waffle cones to go with the ice cream we had after for dessert. "Get used to it sis, and don't ever settle for nothing less" D.J said to me.

I was enrolled in school right away and things felt good inside, finally. The downfall though, I had to listen to my brother and follow his rules, he was now my father figure and the man I depended on. I still can't believe It worked; I swear. He gave her some 14-year-old dick and started to piece his life together. Daniel was so determined he did whatever to reach his goals, next on his list was to get out of his teacher's house. He wanted to be with someone younger, he told me he just rather not have to deal with her anymore but he needed her and he hated that. They would have sex every night and this bitch would also give him straight A's. If they had an argument though, it was real funny because he'd be pissed and secretly hope she'd move a test to the following Thursday after he made up and dicked her down on the Wednesday before. Ms. Lauren though she caught on to his games and would still enforce her rules for school.

"I just need a break from her, something's wrong with the bitch, I can't do this shit no more." D complained to me and she knew there was something up. Daniel barely went to first period and would excuse himself for the rest of the day because of the relationship they had. I began to look at people different after knowing my brother was fucking his teacher. I started to Imagine other shit going on in people's households. Thats when I realized you can't judge someone by their cover but can only view them by the content of which they expose from the inside.

Fortunately, my house was lit. My brother and I did whatever we wanted when we wanted to. Well, I still had to report to him but not the teacher bitch. And when things started to get crazy, it was because bro ain't give a fuck and began to bring girls his own age home. This was never ok to Ms. Lauren, she would be in the middle of cooking dinner and just start slamming pots on the stove. "What the fuck is your problem?" he yelled out to her. "Nothing, I burnt myself." She was lying and just wanted to stop him from flirting with the girl he'd brung over.

What she didn't sign up for though was listening to my bro fuck on another bitch through our thin ass walls. I knew she was getting sick of his shit. One day, she busted in his room while he was fucking some girl and all you heard was, "Get up and get out of my house you disrespectful tramp." She was throwing the bitch's clothes to her and pushing her out the room door then the front door. My bro threw his clothes on and ran up in her face. "Why the fuck you being a hater cus it ain't you in there getting fucked?" "I'm not going to have that in my house." She couldn't even justify it because it was already going on with the two of them. "Bitch you sound dumb, ok cool I'ma let the principal know how often you be swallowing my dick bitch!" I was sitting on the sideline eating popcorn, this shit was like a soap opera. D.J was bad as hell, like Bart Simpson on steroids straight outta control, and this lady was too weak.

You would expect her to say some shit back like ok bitch ass kid, and you gon be back in the system, let's play. Well, that was never her angle, she just let him win every time and I started to believe she had a fake diploma because her ass was not smart, she couldn't be educated and getting played like this. It was obvious what was up though. Ms. Lauren had fallen in love with a teenage boy. His whole thought process for this arrangement was for him to pimp on her, but he wasn't even aware of his pimping at this age. He thought he was just surviving otherwise he wouldn't have gotten rid of her. This lady was for him so much that she was for me. She would do anything he said and people like that are always good to keep around, but he had to learn a lesson from that experience. I used to just sit back and observe it all. I could see his mentality and response towards women change overnight, he was affected by his upbringing. Our mother's death made him view women as weak, pathetic, and so he treated them as such. He also understood that no two women were the same but in order for him to consider you a prize, you had to be in survival mode alongside him. A bitch had to be devoted to his life and not her own, understanding his means to survive was pimping, and you either gon respect it or catch yo cut. He got at every bitch the same exact way, straight to the point, and if they turned to walk away majority of the time, they came back with a different mindset. "If you not sure, then you not ready and I'm not accepting no bitches unsure. You either with it now, or you can try and play catch up later." That was his motto

Sometimes D.J would be super hard on me too. I could take it but more often times, he was mean and not nice. "Can I go hang out with my friend and do homework...?" I'd ask to do simple shit and the answer would just be "No." He was molding me into the person he wanted me to be and I respected him, but I didn't trust him anymore or his process. There was never a reason behind his "no" answer, just "no" and I couldn't question shit. Now I'm looking in the mirror like how can I be great? My daddy issues started right there and that's when I started wishing I had a dad, a real dad. I knew D.J meant me well, but he looked at life differently, especially pertaining to women, and he'd let me know his true feelings about me as often as he could. "You don't fucking listen, you gon be out here like Mel two bullets to the head, dumb as fuck chasing a nigga." D.J felt like I was the rebirth of our mom, and I swear to god, it seemed like the nigga loved me and hated me at the same time. So, I asked him, "When you look at me, is that all you see, a dumb girl?" I asked, thinking he would spare my feelings one time in my life, but I was wrong.

"You dumb as hell. I know what's best for you. If you gon live yo life like that then go get on drugs like aunt Tanya and die," walking out the door he looked back and said, "You gotta do better." Wow He's crazy, that's all I kept thinking to myself, and I grew up confused. Yes my brother got me out the system, feed me, took care of me, but he also mentally abused me, verbal abuse, put me down and belittle me. Am I ungrateful? Was I just a spoiled brat not appreciating his efforts? I was afraid and always trying my hardest to be nothing like my mother, nothing like her sister either, and finally nothing like D.J.

We stayed with D.J's teacher for about a year and a half until he got approved for emancipation and got us our first spot in Oakland Ca. Daniel had been sneaking a girl in and out of his teacher's house for the last six months. It was only a matter of time before he would get caught one day, giving us no choice but to leave, so it was perfect timing.

Chapter 2

Soaking It Up

"Wow bro, is this really our new home?" I asked, barely able to believe my eyes. It was his first apartment, two-bedrooms, one-bathroom, and one room was mine. "You probably were expecting something bigger, but this is all we need sis, just stay focused and I got us." D.J was so convincing and if all I had to do was stay focused, then that would be easy, right? But our home quickly transitioned. Within the next week it was now more like the trap, a kick it spot where bitches, money, and drugs began to take over.

Most of the time, I sat quietly and observed. I would act as if I wasn't listening, like I was paying close attention to the T.V while really, I tuned into my brother's conversation with his hoe. "Bitch, are you dumb?" He asked, and she would always reply the same, "No daddy I'm not." making sure to be extra careful not to say too much. I remember thinking, damn, bro is so good at his role and he knows how to manipulate any situation. The way he dealt with things and how he used an intimidation technique. Then also, there's the mere fact that this bitch needed him and not the other way around. That was the icing on the cake.

He got a few solid bitches on his team over the years and after playing with enough money, D.J sustained a pretty good life for himself at a young age. My custody hearing was coming up and D was ready. It was a long time coming and the process took forever, but today, we were in and out. The judge granted Daniel Jr. full custody of me and we both were ecstatic.

After that, D.J was on one with this money shit selling dope, sending bitches, breeding bullies, and just got his hands on a little bit of everything. I would help from time to time when I wasn't busy with school, but at that time, I was a senior and I really couldn't wait to walk the stage in June. I had a plan and I was for sure gonna run up my money then. I didn't think I'd go to college. After learning the tools of life from D.J, I was already like his assistant or something. Besides, I wasn't sure if he'd let me go away anyways.

Have you ever thought about the mere fact of just knowing someone needs you and how it gives them so much power over you? This is a tool in the game; you gotta be that missing piece. My brother knew I needed him, with no mom or dad, no family at all; just us and we grew up close but eventually this life, this life right here, it will change you.

"Bro you gotta stop this shit, where she gone sleep at?" I said to D.J as he came walking through the door with another bitch, he would accept any girl as long as she came with his fee. This Bitch wasn't even really up to his standards either and hadn't made any real money in her life, mostly because she had too many damn excuses. He had dealt with her before, "she a turn out Nigga!, you forgot?" I was so comfortable saying what I was saying because I was there when he turnt the bitch out. Plus, I figured she already stashed her fee for a while, ran it up, then fagged off on her last nigga to come pay big bro. Cool for now, but this could later on become a problem, she wasn't gone make the cut, no way, not on my watch. "Look bro, if she doesn't bring it in by Friday, she's done seriously." "Alright sis, damn, why you being hard on her? I'm just trying to grab what I can and dump her off somewhere else anyway." He was quick to fire a bitch. "She just gone come back 10x harder" he said walking away. "That's what she better do then because I'm not babysitting no bitch!" I yelled, making sure he heard me as he made his exit. Lucky for me, later that night, the bitch got in trouble for not walking and she didn't really understand his program. She wanted to only play the net, but the net wasn't booming for her at home, at all. I didn't know her real name, but he called her Susie I think you know why. D.J fired her ass that next day. "These bitches gon kill each other," I told D, laughing out loud. "No they not, I'm about to separate all these hoes."

He kept saying we gon get a second place somewhere, a house, but in the meantime we gotta run this money up. He was really in his trial and error stage knocking hoes then dropping them, only keeping the ones of great value. Another bitch came along, and another, and another until finally his first Asian bitch came and really changed his life. She really turned him out got him his first rolie and bussed it down. Really introduced him to some new shit. That's when he expanded, moved me and her into a four-bedroom house along with a 2nd runner up. D.B ... that's what he called her. I would be confused though because sometimes he seemed like he was in love but I think she got it the worst outta all his bitches. The second girl living with us had earned herself a car and could drive me to school daily. She was fresh out of high school so she loved hanging with me. We became hella close, too close let my bro tell it. My new life was starting, I now lived in LA. When we got settled in, there was a million new bitches trying to be the next recruit. D.J was still trying to get things in order back at the spot in Oakland so he made me pick one day.

"Just pick one." I did what he said and picked one girl. I fucked up and picked a weirdo. She wasn't an online type of bitch. D.J was irritated and couldn't do too much posting because it would have been a waste of money. The bitch wasn't even cute enough, so now if she didn't hit off the blade, she pretty much was worthless to my brother, to his team. His girls are mostly dancing in strip clubs, he didn't deal with all the extra shit, so having her was becoming a hassle. I think he began to realize he had hit his max with these girls and was trying something different now.

One night, I heard the new girl crying in the bathroom. "Hey sis, you ok?" I had to ask, thinking to myself it would be rude to just walk by. "Hey, sis yea I'm good, it's just your brother is so mean." "Aww you just gotta toughen up," I said as politely as I could. "I can take it, it's just he can't see that I'm doing my best, this area isn't working for me." I wanted to tell her if this was her best, she needed to go home. I knew being mean wouldn't help so I gave her some game instead. "He only hears your complaints, until you stop complaining and just come home with a bag." "It's not that easy though, I swear." "Girl nothing is easy you wanted to be a hoe right? Get to it then, you got this."

She wiped them tears fast and finished getting dressed for the night. "Sis, I was planning on leaving the house around 10, cool?" "Yup babe that's perfect ... don't come home without a bag." I finished the conversation hoping she was motivated. Her mind was focused and that's really all it takes. To get the bag, you gotta let go of excuses and focus on the winning, focus on the night and it's gone fall in yo lap. This shit's easier said than done.

Around 4 a.m. lil baby came strolling into the front door all cheesy. I knew what that meant. "Yessss Boo, you did it!" I smacked her ass in a congrats type of way, she hit cool that night and came home with her first Rolex on top of $8,000. "Damn girl where was you posted?" my brother's other bitch was asking her a million questions. "I was around." She sounded really confident and proud; shit, I was proud of her. I wondered if she knew she was close to being fired, I turned her up. "Ayeeee you better celebrate that shit, bitch." She was too juiced as well, like don't count me out. I can appreciate a bitch trying. "Ha who getting fired? Not me sis. I'm in my bag okayyyy!" She shouted through the house ready.

I was back and forth between LA and Oakland until I finished school, so I only got to motivate baby sis on the weekends at first. Then she started to call me to talk when she was out walking some nights. We got pretty close and my bro saw how I was influencing her, so he assigned her as my driver to school for some weeks. He said to give my friend a break but really he was hating wanted to separate us, but thats when it would be lit for me. She would hop on the plane and come trap out LA for a month or so. She called herself

Sue and my other friend was SiSi, they would rotate and D.J was coming next. "I wanna come home," I said to my brother over the phone. "Why? You just got there. What the fuck you want?" D.J had just landed; he was tired and irritable, I had just gotten to school maybe a hour ago. I knew he was at the house I just missed him and wanted to go home.

"I don't feel good, pick me up D.J please!"

He knew I was on bullshit but pulled up anyway. "You need to be learning shit." I just ignored him kicked my feet back and eavesdropped on his phone calls. "I gotta pull up on this bitch real quick, meet me up over there." He was talking to his homie and mentioned his bitch wasn't leaving the house because her titties were being done.

The girl he was referring to got her boobs done quicker than any of his other girls because she got straight to it. "My new bitch go so crazy sis, she about to audition tonight and it's over, we getting this money you feel me?" He was talking to me about some nameless girl who go so crazy. While I usually pretended to be annoyed, I was intrigued. I definitely tuned in, and he never really said names to me, but I know their history and current status based off the things he told me. When he finally parked, I hopped out his X6 and looked around to see where we were. I could tell we were downtown L.A it looked so nice outside. We started walking and I noticed all types of bomb ass lofts and arts studios. We got to a pathway that led us to an elevator and from there we went right up to her loft entrance.

"Knock knock knock, open up the door, I'm -at -the- damn -door- let -me- in- Lil bihhh." D.J was making a beat on her door and doing a fake freestyle at the same time. When he was happy, he was goofy and funny as hell. I started laughing as soon as she opened the door. She was laughing too. "Aye this my lil sister, say what's up." He introduced me and nudged me at the same time. Reaching out to grab the door handle behind me, he wanted to make sure he locked the door himself. D would always say you can't trust these bitches nor can you slip up. "Hi little sis, it's nice to meet you." She smiled and gave me a hug. "It's nice to meet you, too. I really like your place. Bro, I want a spot like this." He looked at me annoyed then he replied, "Yeah well you gotta be able to pay the muthafucking rent, plus gas, water, oh and bitch, you using too much water over here!" Shit, I done got him started. I hoped she'd just say ok because his ass is crazy. The girl just sat there quietly; you could tell she was in pain from her new boob job, and had no energy to be fighting with him. I looked at her and whispered, "My bad." She smiled and whispered back, "It's ok" with a wink she got up and walked over to her bag, pulled out a fat stack of money walked to him and sat on his lap. "5,10,15, I'll pull the rest out the bank tomorrow that was my limit." I believe they were talking about $15,000 and now that was chump change to him, one bitch maybe even from one trick, crazy right. "Ok cool, you healing ok?" "Yes, daddy I'm great; I'll be back to work by sat." She was tough, but you had to be like that in this game. It's either you want it, or you don't, you win, or you get lost in the sauce. "Alright let me get my sister back to the house. I'll hit you in a few hours." Before we left, I whispered goodbye to her, "Goodbye." She smiled and waved dropping her head down as she closed the door behind us. It was an uncomfortable feeling meeting her that way, she was another one of his top hoes but there was more to her than hoeing, and I could tell she wanted out, but she wanted the luxury lifestyle. "That's how you check yo trap, pull up check in get yo money, and cut." My brother was in my ear ranting about his money and some other bullshit. Whenever he got like that, I really zoned out in my own thoughts, I was wishing I could help that girl. Maybe she could do something else to help the team; who am I kidding trynna save her, this what she chose. Plus my brother would just laugh at the thought. He was so consumed by the money that he didn't see the bigger picture or even connect with her on another level. I guess because I'm a girl I care too much, but how could I judge him? He's just providing for his family.

About ten minutes later, we were parked and headed up to the next girls house. I rode with him while he made his rounds to about three more chicks. The last girl's spot was literally smack dead on the blade and she had roaches and rats; how do I know? Because I wasn't even going inside to see. "You gon wait right here? It's roaches and rats but you good, they only come out at night." My brother knew how to scare the shit out of me. I'm like a real germaphobe and I wasn't going in no dirty ass house. "No, fuck no, hurry up and take me back home, ugh." He wasn't long, and I told him so when he got back. "That was quick." "Can I ask you something?" I had a couple of things I needed to address. "What blood, ask me." "If all these girls are your girlfriends, what you gonna do when it's time to pick one?" "Girlfriend? These bitches ain't my girlfriends, I don't have no girlfriend. I'm a pimp, this what I do, it's called pimping." "Oh, ok I get it," "Yea and they gotta live separately because these hoes don't know how to get along, and I'm not picking none of these bitches," Of course not, I was laughing in my head. "Well they should, if they all on the same team." He looked at me while I talked but he left me with no reply.

I must have hit a nerve that day because a few weeks later, he started firing hoes left and right. I had that type of effect on him. We could be arguing about something, him being right and me being wrong, but at his own pace he would do it my way pretending to have come up with the idea himself. Even after firing hoes, he still had too many living in separate spots. It was perfect timing when this lady who live around the corner started to rent out her house. It was much bigger a 6 bedroom, DJ hopped on it and paid the rent up for a few months. In the beginning, like every weekend, he would just leave, he had another bitch and another spot that was a flight away, and he kept it like that. I think she was really someone with a hold on him; fuck a bottom bitch, main bitch like when it's all said and done, I think he gon marry this one. He would leave and not say a word, but they knew better than to try and question him either and also knew what to do in his absence. "Get yo ass up and get to it," D would be yelling through the phone sometimes but if you was dancing you knew what days and if you wasn't you had to hit the blade nightly. Even if you hit one night don't matter, the grind was real. Him having all his Girls under one roof wasn't really going well but to separate them all again would take more money, he needed to do something quick.

I was soaking it all up thinking how I could apply any of this to my own life, otherwise it was pointless to be taking notes. I began to figure out that most of the girls who had spots were like independent hoes renegades, flip flop bitches. Sometimes they paid him, sometimes they paid another nigga when they couldn't figure it out. For the girls who did live with him, D.J started giving them bitches homework, goals to hit. This sort of stepped up his pimping by getting them to focus on a target goal, and not the next bitch. One goal for one bitch might be to bring home a better bitch, one that had your own flaw as an asset. Teaching them to embrace that shit really helped his team. One evening a group of his friends came by and brought a few of their hoes. "Aye quit daydreaming and take this picture" D.J said to me. I snapped a picture of a group of pimps with their hoes tucked off in the back. Whole time I was daydreaming I was thinking but who was really winning, the bitches or the guys? The guys were the ones really winning, or nah, was it a prize to be the right man's hoe? All the hoes just stood there quietly watching their own pimp, and they seemed sad in that moment, like pathetic worker bees. I wasn't like them, so I could never judge or even comprehend something I didn't fully understand. They left for a little while to eat and shop. Something was planned for the evening to do as well, so when my brother returned with his girls, they all just headed up to get dressed. This was part of their normal routine anyway, but they weren't going to work tonight. "Where you guys going, you're looking real cute sis?" A couple hours later I said to each girl one by one., as they finished getting dressed. "Thank you; your brother got a table for the weekend; he wanted to enjoy a night out with everyone" Mesh told me, while I played in her makeup. "I always do my makeup after I get dressed" she said. "Oh ok. I wish I could go; you guys always have so much fun, I just have to go to school and be bored!"

I probably was annoying as hell. "Aww babe trust me you don't want no part of this lifestyle, stay ya ass in school and I promise to take you out next year when I get you this fake ID, ok and shhhhhh." She was my favorite, I had known her the longest going on maybe four years, now she was 26, a few years older than my bro. Smarter and cooler, but she still followed his guidance.

A few hours went by and all the same people began to arrive back at my brother's house. This time the bitches were dressed to fucking impress. They looked bomb from head to toe and even more importantly, they looked happy. They looked accomplished and satisfied compared to earlier that day, and that's when I realized it was because they literally all came alive in the nighttime.

Meanwhile, I was trying to stay awake and now it made sense why my brother took a nap with his fat ass. These girls were dragging through the day since normally that's when they are asleep and instead of getting a nap in, they had to take time to get ready to be on point for the evening. That type of commitment and drive was impressive and it was 2 a.m., P hours. The "P" is for prostitution, pimp and profitable money. This was common in Oakland, it's our culture, but L.A I wasn't so sure about. I was watching my brothers Snapchat and Mesh's Instagram story. They were so lit, ugh I think I got a little jealous, but I eventually passed out thinking to myself how I'ma go one day. My thoughts were interrupted "Y'all get inside let me talk to this bitch" I heard everybody coming in the front door quickly, heels click clacking getting up to their rooms. Then I heard my brother come in and he began to yell. "Bitch I can't take yo ass nowhere" "I'm Sorry daddy" "Sorry, bitch you acted a fucking fool and for what? You wanna jeopardize my shit, my name I should beat yo ass huh?"

I jumped up to peep into the living room to see which girl it was, fuckkkk it was MESH! "But it wasn't even my fault dad, I just finished it" Why the fuck would she say that? Oh my God he's about to flip. Him being aggressive is normal but he sounded so mad; I'd never heard him like this. "So you ok with letting somebody get you out yo character? And fuck up our shit, cool leave then bitch cut! Bye" he started pushing her out the door. I'm wondering what the fuck she did so bad to upset him. "Bro chill out, the neighbors gon call the police, what the fuck" I whispered. "Man this dumb ass bitch got us kicked out the strip club, wanna be fighting for no reason then wanna sit here and give me a fucking excuse." I knew that made it worse; she shoulda just said nothing if she was gon play the fault game. He was yelling hella loud, and was drunk somewhat. "Bitch get yo dumb ass upstairs and wipe them tears off yo face!" I couldn't believe he was talking to Mesh like she wasn't shit. "Man, this bitch so dumb. My other bitch working, she see her get mad and they start fighting. I don't give a fuck who started it. Bitch you with me and now you got me hot, they wanna know who I am and some mo' shit so we get up outta there right when police pulling up. Now this bitch crying sorry." He wasn't expecting a real conversation outta me he just needed to vent and calm down. "Damn yea she tripping, you gotta be cool though. Wanna sleep in my room?" "Yea I'ma crash down here." "Alright, I'ma be on the couch if you need me." When I awoke the next morning, D.J had his chef cooking breakfast, the house was smelling so good. I went in my room and saw D.J was up already; he was on the phone telling somebody about his night. "Man that bitch not cool, she gon have to make up for last night, she knew better though." "Yea she outta pocket. How you let another bitch working get under yo skin?" "I'm not fucking with her; she on that weird shit, sent that bitch outta state, she caught her flight earlier. I had to." "Hell yea you did, shit, let her ass know you ain't playing bitch, this ain't for jokes." "Come on bra exactly, told her ass don't come back without 80 or better." His friend was on speaker, they both just busted out laughing.

I left out the room and went to check on the chef. "It's smelling real good over here, is it almost ready?" You could hear my brother still on the phone in the room laughing hella loud, then out of nowhere in a bathing suit, comes his outta state bitch walking down the stairs. Bitch had her ass all out and know damn well she can't even swim. "It smells good babe, oh I woulda cooked for y'all." she looked around and noticed my brother wasn't in the room. "Hey little sis where's he hiding at?" Asking me questions with her fake ass smile. "He's in my room, but he's on the phone," I said pointing to my double doors across the kitchen. "Thanks." She headed to the double doors and opened them both wide "Babe, good morning." "Aye bitch, close them doors, I'm on the phone." I lightly laughed to myself. My bro finally got up and came into the kitchen "Is the food ready, it smells ready?" D.J asked "Almost, big dog, give me about 12 more minutes boss."

"Babe you know I coulda cooked for us" his bitch tried it again. "Cook? The fuck was you gon make? Yo ass can't cook!" I was laughing so hard I started choking on a sausage. "I been practicing and I cook good now." I couldn't take her seriously and even if she could cook, I didn't want none, no thanks I'll pass. She was a sneaky snake type bitch. I'm not sure if that's how you had to be to get ahead in the game, but I didn't trust her nor like her. I kept it cute hi, bye, type shit and made it messy when I wanted to. "Hey when did you get in town?" I was pretending to care when in all actuality, I wanted to know when this bitch was leaving. Not that it even matter, because she always paid what she weigh and one thing for certain, the bitch a heavy weight. This girl so thick, with hella ass and tits. "I'm going for a swim, you guys come out after y'all done eating? And I leave on Monday, cool with you?" She asked before walking away. "Fine by me." I sat there watching, I wanted to see her get in the pool. This bitch don't cook, don't clean, and she fo sho don't swim. "She suck dick tho, suck the shit outta my dick," my brother said out loud to his chef, it was like he read all our minds. I had to exit the kitchen and turn the T.V up. They kept talking about her many found skills, and when it finally hit my brother that his 16 year old sister was present in the room during a dick sucking conversation, he changed the subject."What you watching, Mark?" D.J was walking towards me trying to come take over the T.V."I'm watching none ya." "You lame, you still say that? You need to grow up." He started roasting me while pushing me over on the couch. "Something dang you elbowing me all in my side." We went back and forth. "You not even watching this, yo sneaky ass watching me." He was right I was watching him, just peeping the scene a lil bit seeing what's going on but I wasn't gon tell him that. "Ain't nothing to watch, you ain't no show." "Well this my shit, I'm watching T.V now," he said snatching the remote out of my hand.

He's just a big ass fucking bully. It was his house, I'll take that L. "Tell ya bitch to watch you." I said as I jumped up and yelled before I darted up the stairs. He jumped up behind me trying to snatch any piece of my ankles, but I was too quick. D.J clipped his knees on the stairs trying to lift them back down I was laughing at how out of shape he was. "Hahaha sit yo long ass down old man" I was on a roll with the roast "stomach hanging and shit, you don't need nothing else to eat." D.J was gon fuck me up later, if he wasn't too busy. Later on that evening we all had flights to catch to Oakland. D.j was having a party at the spot out there for one of his girls but for whatever reason, we couldn't find him anywhere. He told all his bitches to be home at 6 p.m. and everyone was on time but him. I knew he was somewhere hiding, I caught him trying to creep past the living room and was headed up the stairs. "What are you doing? You got everybody looking for you." I was cracking up laughing, you shoulda seen his face "Yo ass trying to duck and be sneaky." "Man stop hating and be quiet, I'm about to be back down in a second" he couldn't handle all of the girls together. The ones that lived in the house got along just fine by now, well some days they did, but there were about four that didn't live at the house. At first, D.J had his bitch that was a flight away. D.J liked that idea and began to branch off of that. Now he had two other bitches that live in Vegas in separate houses, one in the Bay and one in LA. These girls didn't like nobody, not even themselves, they had permanent resting bitch faces and were not friendly. You could catch them in a corner somewhere with shades on acting all unbothered. "Just let them mingle for a minute, this what you gotta do. Bring them all together, remind them they on the same team chasing the same bag" My brother was smart and his techniques got him very far, but only so far.

I didn't understand how or why everything was done or what he was missing, but I soon would get it all. We loaded up in the cars and made our way to the airport I was excited to go back home for the weekend. "Cheers to the birthday bitch!" "Eyyy one time for the birthday bitchhh!!" They held up glasses of Champagne to toast for a birthday at the airport bar, and the fun began. Soon as we landed Everyone got drunk as hell and started running through the house like five year olds. They all were like big ass kids, plotting on ways to taunt their daddy, talk about daddy issues.

By midnight, my brother was signaling me to bed, he said it was after hours' time and no kids were allowed. How lame was he, thinking just because they were adults I had to get excluded, like I wasn't old enough to know what was really about to go on. I didn't want to stick around for that anyway ewww, yuck, gross! I think D.J was about to have sex with all of them and I didn't want to even picture it nor hear it, so I did him one better and left for the night. "Have fun, I'll be back tomorrow afternoon." I closed the front door behind me and set the alarm. I had already called an Uber which was pulling up soon as I turned around. I went to stay the night at my friend Jojo's, and soon as I got there, I started gassing my bitch. "Jojo why yo room never clean, what the fuck? Where am I supposed to sleep on yo pile of trash?" She was spoiled as fuck, but they weren't rich enough to be living the way she was living. "Girl bye, you wanna spend the night or no!" "Bitch the maid come once a week not once a day, meaning you still need to cleanup, this is crazy." "You sound like a hater but bitch, I love you too." We both fell out laughing, her dad was in the navy, so they had a little bit of money. "Did you bring the weed or naw?" I snuck some weed out my brother's stash for us to smoke. "You know I got the weed, you got the wine?" We was going to have a relaxing girls' night but Jojo fucked with plenty of niggas, I knew she would find a way to get us into something.

"I got the wine but I don't have nothing to roll up with." "Bitch ok, so let's go to the store." "We can't buy it, we not 18, duh!" "So, now what? Because I need to smoke my nerves bad and my brother and his bitches stressed me out all week, bitch he shipped Mesh off." "What!? Where? Oh my God! Not Mesh, he's wrong, well I can hit up my lil friend to pull up and roll for us." "Uhh bitch is that our only option, because I don't even entertain these niggas?" "Yes, this our only option, so what you wanna do?" She called up this nigga and he came right away with two other guys. We snuck out the house and got in the car.

"Drive up the block, there's a park on the left we can smoke and chill over there." Jojo directed him while I sat in the backseat between two guys trying to play rock paper scissors over a bitch like me though. "What's yo name love?" "Me? I'm Sid, and you guys are?" I spoke to them both ok. "T-rell, and that's Boog." "Oh ok, nice to meet you both." I sat back in my seat hoping they wouldn't ask me anything else. "Y'all wanna pull up to jank shit, he having a party?" the driver asked his friends, and Jojo stopped breaking down the weed to reply for everybody. "hell yes, let's go" he dumped the backwood guts out the car. "Boog roll this" the driver passed the weed and first backwood to Boog then had Jojo breakdown some more weed while he pulled off. I was a lightweight smoker and had only smoked in the house, never out with some niggas. I was a good girl compared to most and Jojo was not. "Sid, you good?" she looked back to check on me, "Yea, I'm good babe, thanks."

These niggas were 20, 18, and 21. Jojo was younger than me; she just made 16. I was going to be 17 soon but I wasn't tripping on their age, just didn't know them at all. Fuck it, I tapped the bottle a few times and poured a shot down my throat. I kept drinking when it came my way and hit the blunt like I was a pro. When we arrived to the party location I just sat back in the middle seat quite as a mouse. "You wanna get out and talk to me for a min?" T-rell was talking to me fucking up my high. "Huh, wha you say honey?" "Honey? Ha come here, come talk to me for a min." He grabbed my arm gently helping me slide out the car; he was fine as hell, but I couldn't catch his vibe. "Where y'all from, the deep?" "Naw I'm from seminary and she's from the dubs." He was gon try and really get to know me I could tell by these questions but thank God some nigga in a jag pulled up. He parked, hoped out, and went right inside. He was fine too but I'm thinking damn he didn't even look my way. I spoke too soon because he got to the top of the stairs and looked back. Checking his surroundings. They all nodded heads saying what's up to each other. Yesss young man, he was more than fine, that nigga was a full course meal with dessert. He had a nice full beard with a white Gucci beanie on his head, diamond earrings, rings on his fingers, and I could see a chain peeking from under his shirt. I walked over to Jojo and whispered, "Bitch who is he?" "Girl I don't know, but I'm trying to find out." "No, you really not sit yo ass right there, you already got a driver." "Bitch rock paper scissors then cuz I'm not going out." She played all day, but this bitch was serious. "Haha blood stop playing; I'm not even in the mood." "Ok rock paper scissors." "1-2-3" boom! I hit. I had scissors her dumb ass had paper. I walked off singing, "He is my rock-ock-ock." "Alright ok, you got me, but if he ain't feeling you, then I'm snatching." "Bitch if, ain't? Ha Byeeee, meet me inside." I walked up to the door and went inside the party. They quickly got out and followed me. I said to Jojo as we looked around and saw that the party was a little all white party, "Bitch I'm so mad, let's leave." She was embarrassed but I didn't give a fuck; I spotted the nigga in the jag; he was sitting in the corner on a shared couch talking to some other girls. "There he goes, what should I do I want him?" At this point Jojo wasn't paying me no mind, she was too busy dancing and doing her own thing, so I had to bust a move quick. I walked over to him and sat on his lap with my back to the bitches and my legs to the right. "Hey, I saw you come in earlier and I just had to come say hi." He smelled so good, his beard his clothes he was clean as fuck. "It's all good love, I saw you earlier too." He was smiling. "So, this how you feeling, huh, like that there?" I saw Jojo watching me; she had my back from across the room and she sent me a text saying, "Bitch are you thirsty or naw?" I texted back, "lol not thirsty bitch dehydrated, hyperventilating, bitch I've lost my breath, fatigue lol is you mad or naw!" We both was dying laughing because that was not something I would normally do. "So, what's your name, where you from handsome?" Now I was being myself. "I'm from Oakland from the dubs." "Oh ok. My girl Jojo from the dubs too. I'm from Oakland as well, what you doing the rest of the night?" "Nothing, about to pick up some shit, drop off some other shit and get some food, you tryna slide?" "Yeah, I can ride with you for a little bit." "Alright get yo thick ass up then," he said tapping my butt being funny because I was only about 100 pounds. We had to make our way through the crowd and on the way out one of the mad ass bitches that was sitting on the couch had something slick to say "who even invited her? That bitch don't got on no white, what the fuck? Like who don't got white?" "ha! Bitch good one I wasn't invited I actually was just leaving." I was holding the dudes arm real tight trying not to rock this bitch dome! "Yea bye please leave. Somebody need to be stopping shit at the door, umm, no trashy bitches in period." She stood near me and tried to sweep at my legs. I grabbed the nigga piece off his waist that I just ran my fingers across and pointed it between her eyes. I know I was rolling off something they had to have put in the Henny because I wasn't even gon stop there. "Bitch I will bust yo shit and nobody will miss you." I said cracking her upside her head, then two pieced her friend standing behind her. "Shut up bitch." We all started fighting then her brother came through bussing at the air like bullets don't gotta come back down. Everybody was strapped and more people started airing it out; I even saw one girl drop to the ground, leaking from the ankles "help me please" she reached for me when I ran passed. I said a prayer and kept it pushing. The nigga had me by the hand bussing back in the direction we was running from because now they were shooting at us. "Jojo run!" I screamed at the top of my lungs. I couldn't see my bitch. I didn't know where she was and I couldn't go back, I just knew she had to be ok. We hit the door and jumped off the top stair, there was Jojo already in the car with the niggas we came with. "Just meet at your house Jo" I texted her she texted back "ok babe be safe" "You wild and shit can't be getting us into no trouble, but I got yo back though" he looked at me smiling he liked that shit anyway and man, that was so typical for a Oakland party, but we rode around for a little bit until he pulled up to the top of 73rd. We went down towards 65th and parked in the hills looking over so you could see the whole view of Oakland. When he finally parked, I asked him again, "what's your name babe, you never told me?" "KC" "KC? I like it, and I like you; thank you for having my back, you a cool ass dude for real." He dropped me off at Jojo's house; it wasn't odd to pull up and see her riding the nigga in the back seat of his car. "Jo his tints are not that damn dark," I texted her as we parked waiting for them to finish. I didn't know if they had history or if this was the first time they fucked or what. "Hey, thank you for everything. We gotta link up again if you want?" "It's all good text my phone right now and

I'ma hit you, I gotta get up outta here though, you gon be good?" "Yes, babe I'm good and ok texting you now, drive safe ok." I leaned in to kiss his cheeks. "Bye KC" he was so chill, just my type of guy. The next day I got home around 2 p.m. and the house was a mess. I could tell they had a blast because they were all still asleep and probably hung over. "I hope y'all called the maid on her day off because I'm not cleaning up nothing." I was stepping over all type of shit. I ran upstairs to find my brother "Aye, D.J where you at?" "Why the fuck you so loud! What you want?" He was yelling from his bedroom. "What the heck happened here? The house's a mess and there's girls passed out everywhere" "Shit we had a lil party, stop asking me hella questions." "A party Nigga? Yo house look like y'all had a riot, and I'm not cleaning shit up, so you better start waking everybody up to help." There was a girl under the covers with him and she started moving. "Yuck, you guys are disgusting and it's 2 p.m. you still looking and smelling like yesterday. She got yesterday's dick in her mouth." "What the fuck you sayyy..." I got a smart ass mouth I knew better too but I quickly exited his room and closed the door to pretend like I didn't hear him, then I yelled from behind the closed door. "I said y'all laying in yesterday sex and she sucking yesterday dirty dick, just nasty!" I ran down the stairs to head to my old room. I got ready to close the double door until I realized there were two bitches in my bed passed out. "You bitches gotta get up out my bed!" I started shaking at their arms trying to wake them, now I'm thinking how high are they and off what. "Get the fuck out my room NOW!" I didn't even know these hoes. They jumped up confused and headed to the living room. I had to have been close to starting my period because out of nowhere I started to cry a little, ugh I hate this shit, emotional ass bitch.

Charter 3

A Pimp's Sister

Shortly after we moved out, Ms. Lauren, started to come back around. Wednesdays were her days, that's when she got done at the school early and could come to the house to clean up and cook. She would always start some shit with bro though because before we'd moved, she got to be with him every day, and it was hard for her to adjust to not having that. She would ask me to talk him into letting her move in, but the place in Oakland was small enough. Most of the bills were in her name, weird shit right? I'd always say, "Ok I'll talk to him." She was annoying as hell and didn't know the rules to this shit, but he could trust her. She wanted to be young and do her at the same time wanted to deal with D.J but other men too. She had the nerve to show up to our spot one day with some nigga. He was some nigga to me, but he was a dude my brother had been fonking with for some time now. Dude's name is Slim, and he tried to knock my brother down once before. Shit went left and he ended up sending D.J's friend to the hospital, nobody took it lightly. Later that week, dudes whole family got knocked off. It was sad but where we from that's how they put their stamp on shit.

When Slim and D.J finally ran into each other, this bitch walked Slim right into his enemy's house. I can't even tell you what my bro did to the dude but after they were done, he had Ms. Lauren drop Slim off at the hospital. She had to say she found him at his own home shaking having a seizure, they paralyzed that boy. The police were all over the shit, so my brother and Ms. Lauren were both hot, and had plans to lay low. Before D.J could get his plan together, the police ran into the house. Now, let's guess who had a gun on them? Correct, it was my brother. I watched the police walk him out the house in handcuffs. "But what crime did he commit officer?" I asked. "We're just taking him downtown for questioning." D.J was so caught up in the dope game and fonking with niggas in the streets that he was letting shit fall off at home. They ended up keeping him and he had no bail. With D.J being locked up, all his bitches were down my throat because anytime they talked to him he would say, "ask my fucking sister. "Stop making excuses and do what you gotta do." So, all these bitches were calling me for every fucking little thing, drama, bills, money, what to dos and how-to dos. I never been so stressed out in my life. "I'm sick of this shit" I was on the phone with my best friend venting about my brother "girl, what is it now, you can't keep being miserable?" "Listen bitch I'm stressed the fuck out trying to keep up with all the lies I gotta make up constantly to cover my bro's ass." "Well stop covering for him." "It ain't that simple." "Yea, it is. Just tell them bitches you don't know shit." "Alright." problem solved right? Wrong. The problem wasn't the girls, it was my fucking brother and his constant technique of involving his sister. He couldn't balance nothing from jail, and I was getting ready to fuck it all up. Everything he worked for.

"I put that on my sister" or "ask my sister she'll tell you" "man, my sister was right there, what I gotta lie for?" Or even worse "my sister a tell you" No the fuck I won't, because I wasn't there and I don't know shit to tell. I wouldn't have the slightest clue about this shit but he's sending bitches to my room all week long with their drama. I had so much better shit to do than to be lying to these bitches about an event I never attended or a trap I never saw. To make matters worse D.J ended up doing 90 days in jail. Punk ass probation violation/hold, I guess they didn't find the gun, I just knew he was going to sit down longer. When they released D he was mad before but now he was pissed and I knew I would need to leave soon, but I had nowhere to go. I stuck around trying to hold things together, I wasn't gon quit on him. I kept telling myself "just thug it out" but it was right back to the drama for him. My last straw was when this bitch approached me and asked, "why did you go to kk's event last week with that bitch who got me fired?" I'm thinking to myself first off, I'm 16 I haven't even been to no club yet. Then I'm thinking is she serious right now, wow she really think I was there. "Yo brother said you was there, you got invited." "I was not there, I don't know what the fuck is going on and I wish people would stop lying on my fucking name." "Why you ain't tell me tho sis, you coulda just told me?" "Bitch I said I wasn't there, wasn't nothing to tell you. I didn't go, wrong sister come again." "You wrong sis," she just kept on going and would not stop."I feel like you working with him trying to hurt me." "Hold the fuck up. I didn't know shit until now, never mind what my brother said, I'm not in this." "But yo bro said you been knowing what was up but you musta went not thinking about her because you forgot." Why in the fuck would he say that? I was trying to end this conversation but here she comes with more shit to dig up. "I'm sorry sis but ya man be buzzing, that ain't what happened. She sent out a regular group text to my group of friends providing information to this event and my friends wanted to all meet there." "Oh ok it's all good I'm not mad, just trying to figure this shit out." "Well you definitely gotta talk more with my bro about it. I'm not sure why he threw me on board with conflict management but that ain't my job." We both started laughing. Normally she's a cool girl, smart, real sweet and means well, just a little dramatic. "So we good then?" She asked. "Yes, we good, shit we great." I wiped an invisible sweat line off my forehead, thank God that's over. I literally dealt with that type of shit about three times per week.

"What's up Tati, where's my bro at?" I asked. "Oh he's out back smoking sis, you all good?" "Yea I'm all good, thanks" Tati was cool too, she believed in resolving all the shit without fighting and to simply come to an agreement, which is easier said than done. "Sid" "yea?" Tati grabbed my arm and told me she was proud of me. "It's not easy being you. I could only Imagine, but I am proud of you girl." "Aww thank you T, that really means a lot." I saw my brother relaxing in a lounge chair at the edge of his pool, firing up his blunt. I wasn't trying to approach him all angry but I had to "Why you keep telling these girls to ask me shit bro? I don't got time and I'm not finna be lying for you no more." "Man, what you saying though? Coming out here hella loud, better ask me again, better start the fuck over!" "Quit telling these bitches to ask yo mutha fucking sister!"

He started laughing "oh I guess you mad, but I don't give a fuck about none of that shit you talking about." "Alright, well, I'm just letting you know that ain't my job and I'm not covering no more." "What you tell the bitch about the party?" "Nothing, I ain't tell her ass shit! Figure it out!" "Man check this out, you not finna be talking to me all sideways"

I loved him because he was my flesh and blood, but I hated him because of the way he addressed me or wasn't able to control his anger for me, his baby sister. I just started walking off in the middle of his sentence before I could step fully back inside, he got up tripping. "Aye lil bitch, you got a smart ass mouth and you fucking hardheaded." "Hardheaded?" What the fuck, just let me leave and get out of here is what I was thinking but I had nowhere to go, and that alone was enough to send me into depression.

"Aye everybody listen up, don't come to me asking about some shit pertaining to my brother, I'm not in it. I wasn't there and I don't know." "Well your brother must be messy. He the one always putting you in it, so we be trying to cross reference since we can't question him but you know what's up." "What the fuck, are y'all dumb or what? First off, I'm a kid, y'all be fucking up my studying time making me fuck up on school projects because I'm stressed out dealing with dumb ass drama at home." "Well we stressed out too." They kept finding a way to make it about them, but this was about me not no dumb ass hoe. "Bitch I'm the one dealing with it on both ends. Listen, I'm just asking that y'all leave me out of it."

"You hella dramatic," one bitch said. "Bitch how? Oh, because my mom dead, and I'm being raised by my pimp brother? What part of that seems like a fucking joke to you?" "I'm just saying you could just be upfront with us about certain shit, that's all." No matter what I said, these bitches believed their nigga as they should, but in return, are getting at me.

I went to my room slamming my double doors as hard as I possibly could, fuck them fake ass hoe bitches. I wanted to slice up everybody. I'ma show this whole house, watch. About an hour later, one by one, everybody began to knock on my door trying to check on me. I'm not sure where the care and concern came from all of a sudden, but shit had to change or else I was going to be a total brat bitch kid. One girl left me a note, some bought me shit like food and flowers, the flowers were my favorite and made me feel a little better.

I put my headphones on and tried to escape into my music. Soon as I began to zone out, my bro had got his spare key to my room and was now sitting in front of me. "What you in here still crying, or you done acting like a brat?" He was awful with this type of shit, anything pertaining to emotions and being sensitive to one's feelings. Yea, it was not his thing.

"I was never crying, and if I'm a brat you're annoying!" Smacking my lips, I rolled over onto my stomach and smashed my face into a pillow. "Just trying to cheer you up, in case you really was in here crying." And there went his apology. If you weren't listening hard enough you'd miss it and he won't go for it again.

That's as good as it gets when it comes to him saying sorry, and I've accepted that. "Well, if it makes you feel any better, I haven't just been up in here crying, I honestly like the alone time." I was hoping he would get the hint and get the hell out. "I guess you trying to kick me out, but I should punch you for all that cursing you did earlier." "Can you just do one thing for me?" "I'm not finna be doing no favors, fuck I look like?" "This ain't no favor, just stop telling these bitches to ask yo fucking sister!" "Man, I'ma tell whoever whatever the fuck I want to, and you better just figure it out." "No! I'm not yo reference. I don't wanna verify shit, I wasn't there I can't back shit up, just leave me out of it please!" "Man, most of the time it be them, so you better talk to they asses about it." "Naw I'm good.

Imma talk to you because you the reason I know them." "Them bitches be needing friends, so they be wanting a reason to come talk to you, that ain't my problem." "Well I don't want to be these girls' friend, counselor, mother, none of that shit. If I got seven hoe friends, won't I be the 8th one?" His eyes got big "man, you ain't finna be no hoe" "you never even thought about that huh?" "Leave me out of it or I'ma hit the streets with it trying to hoe." "Aye that's on you, if you want to be stupid and do that, then best of luck to you." He was sitting in my face lying as if I didn't know he'd send them my way, so he could avoid the headaches. "Alright, I got all these hoe friends I might as well be one; I'll start tomorrow." "Good for you, shit be safe out there" he said as he got up to walk out. "I'm not joking either I'ma be the best hoe, I'ma get rich off this shit and you won't ever get a penny." "Now thank the Game God for that." I added as I slammed the doors shut. I heard everybody laughing like I was some kind of joke. I opened the door back up "Ok, so, what's funny? What the fuck is so funny to you ugly ass bitches?" It was silence. "You know what is funny though, umm Tika, he be fucking the shit outta yo mom without a fee." "What, my mom live outta state you a liar!" "Exactly one of his outta state bitches! And Noonie hmmm, where do I start? He gave you some fake ass Gucci for your birthday because you a faggot, he wasn't gon spend his money on you, plus you can't even make a consistent $800." "You just a lil ass kid who don't know shit about my hoeing." "But that bag fake though, I know that!" She was pissed as hell. "Oh Lizzie you think you special, but you really only got a spot in the house because he waiting on that settlement check and yo dumb ass gon hand it all over too." "Shut the fuck up before I beat yo Lil ass yelling in my fucking house!" "No, you shut the fuck up; I'ma teach you a lesson, you want a bad kid, ok here I go. I'ma get my own house, matter fact two houses, with a nice yard and pool. Fuck you bitches and fuck you too nigga." Next thing I knew I saw my brother cock back his right arm then he released into my chest a couple times. I eventually folded over trying to catch my breath. "Don't you ever disrespect me in yo life, stupid ass bitch, you lost yo mind. After everything I've done for you, this is how you repay me?" He had released a straight monster within me. "You mean after everything I've done for you?" "Bitch I don't owe you shit, you ain't done nothing for me. Get the fuck out my face!" "All your errands, all your back-end shit, things for your bitches, cooking and cleaning up here living like I'm Cinderella with no godmother, meanwhile you wanna play the victim." "You still fucking talking, just pack yo shit and cut!" "Oh, that's exactly what I plan on doing, and I'ma keep talking, ain't nobody gon shut me up, on our dead momma!" "Is that what this is about? Man, grow up and get out yo feelings lil ass baby, momma been dead, get over it." All the abuse I was having to deal with because of his lack of parental guidance and neglect was mentally draining. I needed love and compassion from a real father not my wannabe father-brother. I tried not to blame him, I knew better. It could never be his fault. I know he's affected by his upbringing also and was made responsible for a very difficult task. He was different now most of the time, emotionless, he always said, "you can't work off of feelings, or you'll never accomplish shit." "Bitch, need to get her feelings in check. Aye, put yo feelings back in yo pocket, I don't want them" he wasn't going to let it go just yet, neither was I. "Bitch ass nigga, I don't want you to have my feelings but you gon hear me though." "You think you a nigga or something, you wanna keep raising yo voice, bitch get the fuck out my house and never come back!" "Gladly! Fuck yo house, fuck ya couch, and fuck you!" I flipped him off. "On both my granny's grave, bitch if I die don't come to my funeral, it ain't good!" He walked out to the kitchen and started up the stairs. "Now you nothing to me, I don't know you, we ain't good." I gathered as much of my things as I could and headed towards the front door. Before I could reach for the handle, someone knocked. "Knock Knock" it startled me because I was already in an uproar. I sat my bag down and began to turn the door knob. Someone on the other side of the door let off two shots, breaking the lock bullets missed me by a hair, and these niggas walked right in. I put my hands up "Who the fuck are you?" I said trying to keep calm. "Bitch where the fuck is he?" "Who" "D.J, bitch you know who I'm talking about." These niggas were here looking for him and they wanted blood. I blacked out thinking about a nigga trying to kill my fucking brother, he was gon have to kill me too. Two dudes ran in and swarmed the downstairs area while dude tried to grab me, I sprayed him with mace and jumped on his back pushing his knees in until I broke him down enough to grab his gun. "Daniel!" I screamed my brother's name and shot the dude in the leg. The bullet went straight through and he tossed my little ass off his back. I landed hard on the floor, but I hopped back up to grab the first thing I could. My brother came down bussing his sawed-off rifle; he threw handguns to two of his bitches. "Kill these niggas," he said. There was a lot of shit going on at once, in the back you could see Lizzie with a duffel bag filling it up with my brother's money. "Lizzie, what the fuck you doing?" she didn't say a word, she just kept filling the bag. "Bitch, hello, what the fuck, put that money back." "No bitch, I have to, they gone kill me, they gone kill my mom." Before she could finish, my bro walked up and heard it all. With his handgun, he pulled the trigger twice. She fell and her blood hit me in my face. I wanted to scream, watching her eyes roll and her body go lifeless in a matter of seconds. "What the fuck! Is that her brains?" I yelled out in disbelief. "Turn around and get the fuck out of here, now!" "No! I'm not leaving you, period!" "Man get the fuck outta here, Sydni, you done and I'm not fucking with you no more, I'm cool." "What are you saying bro, really in the middle of all of this?" "Man, leave! Get the fuck out, go live yo life!" "Fine then I'm gone, hope you make it out this bitch alive." I wiped the tears falling down my face and walked straight out to the living room, everybody fired shots but that's when I knew I was protected because I was prepared to die at that moment.

D.J was the first man to break my heart. I didn't understand and even in the moment, he was still completely heartless. He ain't give a fuck if I was dead or alive. I couldn't worry about him no more; he made that clear but one thing about my brother if you come for him and he didn't send for you, he's not going to go without a fight. Him and his girls killed everybody and got up outta there. "Call the old bitch who name this house in, tell her get over here now, tell her she gon say she just came home, and her house was on fire." Police didn't bother to come when they heard gunshots where we from, so it worked out perfectly. "When Ms. Lauren get here, blow this fucking house up." D.J said, hopping in his car and leaving everything behind. I had to hear about it in the streets because I left before it ended, I spent a few years in that house, now it's gone.

I had nowhere to go and I wasn't sure if I could figure this shit out. A part of me thought I should stay, but these niggas had been trying to kill each other for months now, and ain't no telling if it's over. I had to get the fuck and start my own life. Plus, D.J made me leave, now I ain't have a choice. I still had my car thank God, literally half way through me packing, he started yelling out a list of things he wanted back. He yelled, "Aye bitch, bring me all yo bags and anything else, designer shoes, belts, and wallets." This how he would get a hoe bitch, the same way he did me. I mean, talk about breaking you down or kicking you when you're low. You know how bad I wanted to say sorry and just start over, but my pride wouldn't let me. I was thankful he let me keep the car because that was my whole house. There wasn't no going back after this though, and if I said sorry, he would laugh in my face and really make an example out of me. I pushed myself to keep driving, knowing I had to leave before the situation got worse. I was tired of being in the middle of stupid shit, this shit was petty as fuck and I'm always the bigger person but not today, I wanted to act my age and some. My heart flooded with hurt and regret, but was I wrong? He was using me to his advantage. One time, this girl and I even had a fight because he put me in some shit. A girl came into the picture, she was maybe 18, but long story short, he told her, "Ask my fucking sister." She replied, "Oh, that bitch knew about this too?" Minutes later, she rushed my door with her body and it popped open,

71

she immediately jumped on my bed and started drilling my shit, hitting me in the face. She had caught me off guard, so my brother wanted a rematch. "Bitch, you could never see her from the shoulders though, let's get a rematch." Soon as he said that she stopped talking, and I was just trying to figure out why we was fighting in the first place. My brother used that fight as a tactic, and he would tell his hoes something like "Bitch stop playing with me before I have my little sister get on you." And most of the time, a hoe gon bite into it, "Oh, well go get that bitch." He would never go get me to fight but this created bad vibes for me. Bitches was mugging, bumping me as they pass by, but I learned how to not respond and eventually they would let it go. Everybody always talked about the fight video. If you wasn't there that day, you still saw it because he made sure to send it to every single one of his bitches. D.J was kinda messy too if you ask me, sending the video around so everybody knew the bitch got her ass beat. Oh, and not to mention, when the fight was over I did say, "Oh, well bitch, yup I knew," which made the shit no better, but truth was I didn't even know. I was just trying to help my brother.

Sometimes I would think that my brother would forget that I was on his side, or forget that I wasn't a hoe but his sister. He had me fighting, but I was never equivalent to her. "How dare you put me in this type of drama?" I got up yelling at my bro, but one of his hoes was yelling over me. "I can't do this anymore. I'm done I want out!" She was crying so hard because she didn't want to let him down, but her course was over. He ignored her and stayed on my helmet "Bitch you just said you ain't give a fuck, yea you knew." He was delusional believing his own lies. "Are you dumb? I asked "dude I'm just talking shit, saying anything I didn't have anything else to say., but we all know that is not what really happened" I told him I was tired of covering his ass. Shortly after I ran to my room, I could hear him saying "Yea I didn't even know they was close like that, she shoulda just told her and I woulda responded." Lies! My brother was a straight cornball with this shit. There were so many other occasions he used my name as a reference point, to basically vouch for him. Those days were done.

I couldn't be chasing after my brother and his hoes. He had expected me to be different, but I was me and for whatever reason, that wasn't working out for me under his roof.

I put a hotel in my Google maps and planned to just stay there a few nights, I was thinking of calling my friends, but I knew better to do so. They all hated my brother because we be so up and down and shit, things change; we could be cool one day and off another. I knew this was something I had to overcome on my own. I had to focus because I didn't ask for this shit to happen. I had done my best by my brother for years, it was time to do my best by me.

Chapter 4

The Interview

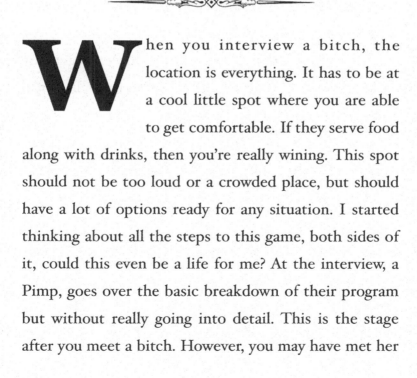

When you interview a bitch, the location is everything. It has to be at a cool little spot where you are able to get comfortable. If they serve food along with drinks, then you're really wining. This spot should not be too loud or a crowded place, but should have a lot of options ready for any situation. I started thinking about all the steps to this game, both sides of it, could this even be a life for me? At the interview, a Pimp, goes over the basic breakdown of their program but without really going into detail. This is the stage after you meet a bitch. However, you may have met her but you're uncertain if you really wanna lock her in. She may not be a good fit for you, that's why you have the interview to see where her head's at, see what type of plans she already has made for herself, and if she's willing to change all that up.

"We finna get to this money though, that's what you here for right?" You don't have to use these exact words but in brief, that's how you get straight to it. Well, this is what I know about the game. You can't even play with a bitch and let her think otherwise, or you'll end up in a relationship with a hoe because you thought you were pimping. There's a lot of hoes out there that want more. These girls want to fuck for money, have a boyfriend, and be in control all at the same time, how that work though? If and when a guy slips up or isn't really a pimp, any real hoe gon know right away and will take full advantage; I promise you. A lot of pimps will let you know right away, ain't no B.F.E, and that's the abbreviation for No Boyfriend Experience. I feel like pimps took this from the girls because it's actually a service to offer G.F.E, girlfriend experience. Some tricks want this, and it consists of kissing and holding hands etc. With this interview though, you really just have to get straight to it because if you're only looking for a hoe at that particular moment, you need to find out right away if she's with it, then she can still ride with you, if she's not, then end everything. No point in moving forward with someone that ain't trying to be on your team. Your time is very valuable as a pimp and the only way a hoe gon respect it is if it's something you live by. You can't be half ass with it in the beginning because that's when you're building your trust and really getting personal with your first hoe to keep it afloat, you have to maintain a good flowing relationship with this girl first. Some people will try to say you're mean or whatever, but if you're chasing that bag, getting a broke bitch who's going to waste yo time out the way is always a good thing. This is what I respect the most about the game, the hardcore, realness, tough love type shit, because a good pimp really won't steer you wrong. A good pimp is looking out for your best interest, so sometimes they might say some shit that comes off as mean, but they only trynna prepare you for the game because it ain't nice. Ain't nothing about it easy either. So, once you get everything understood with the bitch, you can't hesitate to get your fee because for one, it's gone look like you're a rookie. (Even if you are, don't expose your hand. You really gotta fake it till you make it.) A bitch only gonna pay you if you can be an asset to them, a father figure, or like her mentor. She expects you to be a seasoned pimp and know your way around in the game, having expectations for her and being able to take control of her life immediately. Once you got the fee it's a done deal, signed and sealed, she fucking with you now. Her fee could be money from anywhere like a hidden stash she been adding to for months, or her trap from the previous night. I even met a bitch that gave her hair and nail money up as her choosing fee, left her last nigga thinking she was coming back with a new weave. These bitches are relentless and will find a way to come up with it if they really want. If a bitch got a hidden stash, that mean she's been peeling money off after every date, and that's cool she did that and came to fuck with you, but you gotta be very aware of it and know that there's a possibility she'd do it on your clock too. Once the ball is in your court, put a stop on all games because the next nigga could be holding your trap the same way you just was holding dudes' before you. You gotta get her phone, see what regular men she's been texting, meaning men who ain't tricks including her last pimp, you gotta serve him his papers and make sure to inform her that if she get caught up talking to a nigga that ain't paying for that shit, then she's gotta go. Pimping is just like having your own business, and there are rules, but some get bent by you the boss, and or altered accordingly. No two pimps are alike, and you can expect nobody to follow rules from back in the day because the times have changed, and you gotta stay elevated in order to maintain shit. The only way to succeed is by customizing your business, making it unique so that others are curious about your play book. Don't make your business so accessible, let it be a desire or a dream for women to be a part of what you're building. I've heard so many stories about the process, or in other words, the point or step right after you think you knocked the bitch. You just simply seal the deal but before all of this, initially, you have to shoot your shot. If you want it, you gotta go get it or wait till it come to you. This part is where most men get separated. Either you got it or you don't, and you'll know quickly while trying to shoot your shot. Most niggas hang themselves because they're either too shy or don't come off about their money. This ain't something that can really be taught, you just either got it or you don't. You gotta make that first impression a lasting impression. Give her something to look forward to, otherwise what separates you from the rest? Depending on the hoe or girl, you can't even be too nice because some hoes are used to being pimped a certain way already, so if her last pimp kept her ass in a cage, that's exactly what you need to do, otherwise you ain't really pimping in her eyes. If you're too nice opening doors and shit, they gon take you as a joke and may never pay you because you look to weak and too thirsty for it. There's so many different type of pimps. You got flashy ones, you got the ones who talk that talk, "Yea baby I'ma playa, fine nigga from the Himalaya" it be sounding so lame but they really exist. I be wanting to say shut the fuck up, but at some point and time that worked for them, so they kept at it. You would be surprised at how many bitches will put you in the game unaware that they're doing so. The best kind of pimp though is a non-rehearsed nigga, just doing him comfortably. They be encouraging and will show you how they changed a bitch life not afraid to invest in their bitch. Social media is a great way to jump start yo shit once you ready to be all in with it. These women will see because it a show on your social media, and they will get at you outta curiosity. You gotta kinda do the interview process over the phone depending on if the girl outta state, so that way y'all talk about her flying in but know off top what's going on when she arrives. It's a big ass finesse. Honestly, niggas tell a bitch anything to get her to pay and that ain't nobody business, but you gotta be careful not to give up your game and or program to a sneaky bitch. She really ain't supposed to know shit. The right way to do it is have yo bottom bitch screening calls or hire a phone girl, and when the bitch ready, she ain't ready till she in yo face dressed ready to go, fuck getting ready. Thinking shit through before you even get started because you can avoid a loss, but you can also walk right into one; it's to choose whether you paying attention or not.

I met this renegade hoe when I was out one night, and she just kept talking about last year, telling me stories about shit she did last year, how much money she made last year. She claimed shit hit for 80 bands; I'm just thinking like ok cool, yo team should be up still then, but she was raggedy as fuck. This ain't no game, you can't just tell people anything. Muthafucks wanna see where the proof is, otherwise you ain't talking 'bout shit. I told that bitch straight up, "Judging by your current situation, sounds like you had a good team but you just a fag now, right?" "I ain't fag off, I mean, I left when I made my money because I had other plans." "Exactly, you just fucked off some money that was deserving to a real bitch and ain't got nothing to show for it." The Bitch started crying. "I tried everything, he won't even take me back now." She was young and didn't know any better; she just jumped into the game thinking she was gon bend the rules. Naw lil baby, you need guidance, now you regret that shit, that's crazy. Once you fuck over a good pimp, ain't no getting back because he's got too much to lose. She either fucked over a good pimp, or he wasn't paying her no mind anyway and probably didn't even know she hit, it really be like that. These bitches come and go, the real prize is in staying down. Bitches jump in the game fresh 18 like they got all the answers, but you gotta be able to follow directions and be a team player in order to succeed. It's a whole plan step by step followed by the process, and I mean literally, a pimp is like a scientist. He plays with the shit until he get that right combo to make the volcano erupt. Mixing up locations, fixing up ads, changing up the phone girls, helping create the girl's new name and look, there's so much that goes into it, ain't no easy task. Your hoeing gon follow you too, you definitely get a resume when you first start and you gotta build that shit up but at the same time, stay put like you a put a year in at a job to get a raise or to be approved for a loan, same shit like how long was you down for your nigga, did you have a new nigga every month? That's how each pimp gon perceive you if you come their way of course, they will do their part, but in the back of their minds will always be a mental note of what they suspect you to be "you a fucking faggot" Once you're stamped with this, nobody gon take you serious, they just gon check whatever lil change outta, you but you'll never be an investment. After all of this, it finally comes down to one thing and one thing only... can you hoe? Like no breaks, feet to the pavement, all money in, real life hoeing. Do you have regulars on deck? Sites? Any good reviews? How independent have you been? Are you an asset? If you can't get the money you came for, are you gon rob him in his sleep? What type of finesse you come with, because there ain't a hoe walking this earth that's just hoeing, you gotta come with it. It's so many bitches fucking for $50 that the game is real competitive. How you gon break the bank? What technique you finna use? Not one hoe come perfectly put together, every bitch got a catch to them and after that first night of pimping, you will stumble across that shit and now you gotta mold a bitch into your liking, straight build a bitch. Grasp her thought processes and start teaching her shit so that she's beneficial to you. As a pimp, it is your job to get a hoe going, motivate her, train her appropriately. You gotta enable her mind to not only see your vision, the bitch gotta understand it and help take it to the next level, but is she trainable? Otherwise she's in the way. Don't matter how you get it, just get it and bring home new bitches. Depending on your finesse, a lot of times you ain't even gotta fuck, just be close and touching but then a lot of hoes be fucking cuz they actually like to have sex. A lot of hoes hustling backwards and would be better off getting a 9-5 because that's exactly what hoeing is if you ain't making no real money. You hustling backwards because you spending everything you make, ain't no point in hoeing. Most of the time a hoe is just a fast hustler, impatient. Needing that bag quick that's easy, but to master it and create long term relationships with your tricks is a more profitable business.

When you work a job, you calculate gas or bus fare, food for lunch etc and if it don't add up, you ain't gon take it right? Same shit applies with hoeing. I learned early that life was all about the game, no matter what your profession is, your boss is pimping you. Think about it, you're working hard, building his brand, you're apart of his team, and most of the time, you'll never meet the company owner. Once I realized this, I started thinking, ok you either a pimp or a hoe in life, but how do you choose? If you see the roles and understand them both, then you would have a difficult time choosing because there's good and bad in both.

I can appreciate hoeing for what it really is, and not what society tries to influence you into thinking it is. It's not all just sex and drugs, fucking dirty ass tricks, and getting STDs. I know bitches hoeing that are clean as fuck, pussy never stank and she paid, more paid than a bitch working a 9-5, fucking the same bum nigga seven years, done caught a gang of STDs from her one nigga. Then I know bitches that are escorts or dancers breaking the bank nightly, and ain't gotta do much of nothing, just bossed up. Can't forget about the lil bitches that stay at the doctor's with an STD because they sucking and fucking hella dirty dick niggas, trynna figure this shit out. I know hoes who love themselves and ain't just fucking for a bag, nah they fucking for a house or they gotta whole family to feed, I respect those type of bitches. They bend the rules and create their own money outlet from sending videos, to sex calls, all type of shit besides fucking. A bitch that can get on the phone and tell a trick she needs 10 bands and he gon do it with no hesitation, that's an incredible bitch who built up her resume, got good reviews and shit, a nice body, it's a nigga in her ear for sure. If you redefine the word hoe according to these bitches, the definition ain't equivalent to the term they produce. These bitches are smart as fuck; they figured out a way to manipulate the game and make good money and this is why I had a hard time choosing. Thinking about this will have me stuck for days, and going into the perception of a pimp is definitely not fair. The way the world labels a pimp is something awful, you automatically get viewed as the gorilla pimp beating a bitch ass, forcing her to sell her coochie against her own will. That ain't the case, these bitches be wanting to hoe and a real pimp don't wanna be bothered with you unless you got your mind made up anyway, because time is money, if he's wasting time trying to convince you and not getting paid, then something ain't right. The hostel environment usually comes from boyfriend pimping. When you have all your bitches under one roof, you'll experience a few fights and temper tantrums, but over small shit like reminding a bitch to wash her dish out or keep her room clean. Other than that, these hoes should be organized, and ready to get to it daily; it's a must. A pimp can't always be the bad guy, either these hoes be pushing buttons after coming into it, a bitch be careless, homeless, phoneless, and got the nerve to be ungrateful too with her hungry ass. Like bitch you starving every day all day even when I'm keeping you fed, and I still gotta hear yo fucking mouth. That's when you push a pimp and he either gone snap or just wash his hands with you, because at the end of the day, you gotta come into his environment and offer some peace, some new shit, some shit that makes you unique, not just arrive falling apart, needing all types of help. Don't need bitches like that to even be around, but some pimps be nice and understanding. That 30 days rule has to come into effect quick. These pimps, they come across bitches on drugs, alcoholics, but will help her kick that shit, then motive her and boss her life up fully. That's if you got a patient pimp, though niggas be in it for themselves, always remember that. The real definition of a pimp is someone who protects and provides guidance, a leader of his own team. While some niggas be pressed literally sweating the bitch, they fuck it up for all pimps making the title of a pimp seem lame. With that being said, the same question for a hoe applies to a pimp, are you a good pimp or a bad one? What are you investing your money in? Are you fair to yo bitches, or is this a game I got caught up in?

Some of these dudes been pimping for years and only thing they got to show for it is some designer that we can't even tell if it's legit or not. Not even a car owner nor a renter, just on feet winging it day by day and could knock a couple cool bitches in the right environment. If you don't do anything else, make sure to invest in your bitch, uplift her, believe in her, and most importantly, don't put your hands on her. Beating a bitch ass will affect yo money because now she all bruised up, possibly got a black eye, and her makeup ain't gon cover that shit so she gotta sit down for a few days. After sitting down a few days, she liked that down time and decides hoeing ain't for her, now you lost a bitch all because you couldn't control your temper. Now every day it's a fight to get her outside. You can still be scary without hitting her all you want, but never put yo hands on a bitch, ever. An argument could even fuck up the flow of her night, so when she come home empty, it's because she going through it at home, and it shows. At the end of the day, what matters is the outcome, the credit and blame all goes to the pimp. Thinking to myself how I could be a pimp, or was that even an option. Wait, but I would have to trick girls and fuck them pretending to like them. I mean girls are cool, though I never really considered fucking with one, I mean a bitch could eat my pussy. I think pimping might be too complicated for me, if I'm expected to be the brains of the operation, how's that gon work? Why the fuck am I tripping so hard? Ain't nobody's business what I decide to do. I gotta choose whatever is more convenient for me, I gotta pick right now, fuck later.

Chapter 5

Pick a Side

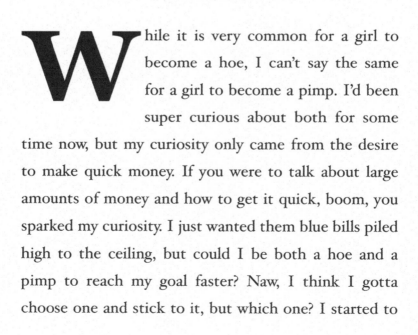

While it is very common for a girl to become a hoe, I can't say the same for a girl to become a pimp. I'd been super curious about both for some time now, but my curiosity only came from the desire to make quick money. If you were to talk about large amounts of money and how to get it quick, boom, you sparked my curiosity. I just wanted them blue bills piled high to the ceiling, but could I be both a hoe and a pimp to reach my goal faster? Naw, I think I gotta choose one and stick to it, but which one? I started to think about my demeanor and my personality; could I really see myself getting on stage at some club dancing for mostly one dollar bills, busting that shit wide open for a stranger? Everybody had already thought I'd resorted to hoeing by now, I'm sure of it. I was tired of muthafuckas trying to count my pocket wondering how I made my cheese. I kept to myself, so people could never really figure me out. My mentality towards it all though was fuck 'em, fuck everybody. They were looking at me stack up my little change thinking I was making big moves, but I wasn't even getting a lot of money, I had babysitting gigs paying $100 a night, but what's that compared to some hoe money?

I'm the type of bitch that's gon go all in with the shit. If I'ma be a hoe, shit gon change drastically; I'ma be counting up bands, not playing with no ones and fews. I've seen hoes count up two to three bands a night, on a bad night. That's what they would call some change or some fuck off money, because it wasn't shit; they had rent in that amount, even cars that cost more. If I was gon hoe, I wasn't gon play, baby I'ma go straight to the top, period. I know bitches sucking dick $50 a pop, though I for sure didn't want that type of life, that could never be me. Shit, I don't even like sucking dick so you definitely gotta pay me enough to even get it poppin'. I think I would probably like it if I had a better technique or a better nigga's dick to practice on. Shit all I know is, hoe money for sho money, and I needed to get to it Who was I kidding though, I mean honestly my mentality was so different, I admired the hustle of a hoe. The fact that a bitch could wake up daily and get to that shit, I admired the tunnel vision of it, and how bitches could just zone out for her pimp, and or the bag. Whichever they chose to help them escape the reality of getting fucked by different men, they zoned out and went hard at that particular task. I've been in that room before, several times and no matter how you spin it, drunk, high, or sober, it ain't no easy task. I would plan to make the trick nut on sight, like I just had this amazing body that he'd look at me, get so horny and cum all on himself then I'm out the door. I probably seen that shit happen in a movie but in real life, you could make the nigga cum quick and be done in like five minutes. Touch the nigga leg while you climbing up towards him and he nuts before you have to do anything. I've heard many stories of that or even giving him a massage before sex, and he nuts and you're all done. See, that type of shit had me thinking, ok I could finesse my way around it, but you gotta have that confidence and take control of the room. You gotta be sexually experienced and know how to seduce or play little games with the body and mind. I didn't want to be getting fucked, but if I was gon be a hoe, I had to be the one doing the fucking to make sure I was timing it and getting it over with quick. I've studied this game for a long time now, watching pimps figure everything out. I know the ins and outs, from when you step foot into the door, you greet them with a hug, your money should be on a table or night stand ready for you. When you grab it, put it away, step into the restroom let him get comfortable; come out and get to it. You can't even be nervous either because they will know right away, from your body language and behavior. Sometimes they be more nervous than you, and that's just a bad mix. You've gotta really try and set the mood and be ready for whatever comes. Most girls get high or take a few shots. If you get to the point where you just can't do it and you've gotta chicken out, try to leave with something. I snapped out of my thoughts, Ok I've decided, no more playing, I'm just going to head to Frisco and go from there. I parked at a paid lot not too far from the hotels and stepped right inside to meet my first trick. I started to plot on him, he's an older Indian man. I was minding my business standing by the elevators when he passed me saying a name several times. "Sasha, Sasha is that you?" sounded like Sidney to me so I replied, "Yes, it is, hi." I was nervous, so nervous I jumped right into character thinking, ok gangsta, let's do this. The guy was extremely nice. He said, "Ok let's go up, have some fun, then we will eat dinner later." We got to his room and he began to undress, "Just let me take a quick shower my love, to wash away the day, I'll be right out." It was so gross, pimples on his hairy back, pear shaped legs, and I could smell his ass juice on his dirty drawers. His butt was so flat it almost looked like it got sucked in with a suction cup. I had to hold my breath trying not to gag. I replied, "Ok baby, take your time; I'll be right here." Whoever this Sasha girl is would be mad as hell knowing I just slid in on her trick like this, oh and I'm finna break the bank too. The funny thing about this shit is if you want it bad enough it will come to you. I mean like really manifest your thoughts I hadn't posted no ad or nothing I just was on shit at a random hotel. While dude undressed I was thinking and creeping at the same time. He stepped into the shower and I crept to his pants pinching my nose to avoid the smell. I slid his wallet right out and took everything but his ID. I quickly grabbed my bag and exited his room, careful not to let the door slam. I could hear him calling the name "Sasha, are you here still?" I darted to the elevator and went down to the lobby floor and there she was I saw Sasha. Everything went in slow motion and them laws of attraction was kicking in because I swear, I was thinking this shit as it played out step by step. When I was upstairs pretending to be her, I kept saying I want to see her. I wondered what she looked like and now I was face to face with her, she was bad as hell, tall also but not quite my height, and her complexion was a little bit darker. She had some cool size titties too. This bitch is like Ethiopian or Eritrean because that's the only similarity we got. I had people stopping me all day, Monday through Sunday, asking me if I was one or the other, and I even had people come up to me in the coffee shops speaking the language as if I could understand to reply. Fuck it I said thinking quickly as I went for it. "You're very pretty. Are you Eritrean?" I asked her as I passed by. She started walking with me, "Yes, I am, how did you know? Are you from Eritrea also?" "No love, just a lucky guess but your eyes really gave it away." She started smiling and we hit valet area, so I stopped walking thinking I would say goodbye, but her body language was telling me she wanted to come. "What's your plans, you busy or you free?" "Oh nothing, was meeting someone but they didn't show up, so I'm free now." "But do you normally cost, because I'm sure niggas wouldn't mind paying for that shit?" "Ok wait, I'm not free ever but I made an exception for you today." "Yea I like that a little better, let me know it then." "Are you staying here at this hotel?" "Yea I was, but I just checked out about to go grab some food. You coming?" She replied, "Yes." Boom, I got her. D.J told me a good bitch gon look good, well kept, she gon smell good too. This was my first time, so my excitement was real but I'm not even gay though, what the fuck! Damn, how I'ma spin this? Well, I really ain't gotta fuck her ever, I could just keep starving her right? But if she a goer, I gotta fuck to put my stamp on it. Sex creates that bond and attachment, I needed that to be created to even begin to build with this bitch. I'm thinking so far ahead but I don't even know her yet, let me just calm down and see how this shit plays out today first, because she could be a bum bitch who knows. "Are you from the city?" "Naw, I'm from Oakland. What about you?" I could tell she was just trying to make conversation, which was cool though. "I'm from Portland." "Moved out here for?" "Tryin to get my money right, working you know." "So how it's been going for you?" "It was cool but now it slowed down, was waiting for it to pick back up or I was gon change locations." "Yea that makes sense. Gotta pay attention to the seasons and the events, you move when they move, feel me?" "Yea definitely." "I gotta make a stop real quick." "Ok" I pulled up to this one hoe house that I met through my brother. I watched her kids often but she owed me, I figured it would be a good look to handle some business in her presence. My brother said to always affiliate yourself with money and show a bitch that you get it with or without her. I bounced out the car and texted the bitch to meet me downstairs. She handed me the money she owed and a tip for it being late. "Alright hit me up later." I made my way down the stairs kinda fast paced to the car. "Ok, ready to eat now?" "Yup yup." I know I have the starter pack, a car, some money, I'm fresh with a designer bag and I knew plenty cute bitches, I'm fully affiliated. We pulled up to this restaurant and went inside. Now I found myself sitting in a room with a stranger preparing for the interview process. I never interviewed a bitch before and this part of the game I didn't get a chance to observe, being that it's more of a one on one type vibe. I just started asking the bitch some random shit questions like, Who you live with, what's your age type questions, because now I was thinking about what I was gon do with her, all depending on her age and location? She was 21, perfect! I needed to hear that shit. I was only sixteen, but wasn't gon be none of her business either. I was so caught up in the interview I didn't realize how horrible the service was. Forty-five minutes went by and not one waiter came to our table to offer us no water, no bread, not even a utensil. "What the fuck, let's go." "Ok." We both pushed our seats back and got up from the table; as we began to leave, some workers rushed us at the door as if we were eating and dashing. They tried to block us in, I got so upset, "Would y'all move, we ain't do shit. Come on love, go straight to my car." I had to let her know we not stopping, we not entertaining shit. She jumped into the passenger seat of my Benz and we took off to look for another chill spot.

I woulda been screwed if my brother took the car back, out here looking like a lame bitch but even beside having my car, I had all the necessary tools to jump into this game.

I pulled up to the 4-8 taco truck because the bitch claimed she knew something about Oakland, so this was her test for a couple different things. The blade was right here at the taco truck; I wanted to see if she was familiar with it, if she knew how to play it. "How much cash you got on you so I can grab these tacos?" I didn't have any cash, and I still wouldnt have paid, absolutely not. On top of that, I wanted to see how bad she really wanted to fuck with me, or if I was going to have to tell her to give me my fee. She pulled out this white Michael Kors bag and gave me everything in there. "How much is this?" "$12,000" "This everything or you got another stash somewhere?" "Yea that's everything." She looked at me with a smirk. "Oh wait, here's this for food." She pulled a $100 bill out her titties. "Rainy day stash?" I said trying to make a joke. "Yea, well like emergency stash." We both started laughing because $100 wasn't gon get you too far in case of an emergency. "Hopefully I'm in good hands now, and you can do all the stashing." "Definitely , got us!" She felt real comfortable and relaxed with me. I liked that about her more than anything, just knowing she was really being herself and giving her all was priceless. I was feeling her but wondering why this shit was super easy, like she fell from the sky, well-seasoned, walking around looking for a bitch like me? Hell naw, what's this bitch catch? I had to figure her out sooner than later because I had no time to be playing.

"You like green sauce?" "Yea, did they give you some lime too?" I took two pieces of the cut-up lime for myself then handed her the bag with the rest. "Yup. Here you go." We both ate silently and when I thought she was close to being finished I asked, "Anything else you wanna tell me?" "Anything you want to know babe?" "Shit I really want to know everything, you got time for that?" Hit her with some fly shit, she responded quickly, "Yes, I have all the time for you." Boom she was now officially my bitch. I reached over and grabbed her phone that had been ringing for hours.

"You gon take this call, let this nigga know you busy or what?" "That's him, he keep on calling wondering where I'm at," she replied. "Alright let me handle it." I answered on the next ring. He instantly hit that FaceTime button, I answered and let him know exactly what it was, introduced him to some pimping he wasn't ready for. "Man, bitch put yo nigga on the phone," he said as he laughed unimpressed and confused. "Look don't hit this phone no more, matter fact you can keep calling we coming new anyway, but this is what it is, she choose up better luck next time P." I held the wad of cash to my other ear, showing him what it was and then I hung up the phone. I know he was mad but that's the rules of the game, sorry boo that's how it goes. She just looked at me with a sexy grin like she was hella turned on or something. "You like that type of shit huh?" "Ummm I guess, why you say that? What made you just say that?" She asked. "I can tell by the way you looking at me now, you was giving me a look before but now, you giving me that I'm ready look." "Oh, is that what I'm doing? I had no idea I just thought I was peeping the scene or something."

I ain't never had no pussy before so now I had to pretend like I had this gay shit to a science. "Yup, so go on keep telling me." "Ok baby I can do that." I took her back to my hotel room where I had some weed already pre-rolled and ready. "Huh, hit this." I said after taking a few hits off; I had a feeling she would say some weird shit like she don't smoke, so I didn't even ask just passed it to her with no choice. You gotta have that type of control mentally and physically building a bitch up to your liking and standards. She broke me off my first bag and gave me some pussy for the first time. I didn't even know what to expect but I knew I had to remain dominant and in control, but before I could order her to do something, she was all over me giving me a little baby massage caressing my titties. I could see her mouthwatering, felt her pussy throbbing on my thigh as she sat on top of my leg; she was feenin' for this shit. "You smell so good, you just smell like you got money, can I taste you?" On gawd, I wanted to laugh so bad, I even thought about pinching myself because I knew the possibilities. I knew where we could go with this game if only I'd knocked the right bitch and boom, falling out the sky is the right bitch, just right for me. "I'ma let you taste me but you gotta go crazy with this money right after you done tho, alright?" "Ok bet, that's easy baby I'ma show you." I wasn't sure if I made a deal with a bitch running out of luck or if she was really a goer, I just made the deal and put my tittie in her mouth. "Perfect, you ain't gotta talk about it love just show me." She obviously had been with bitches before because she got active on me real quick. She wanted to feel my pussy, she kept saying, "I want to mix our juices."

She started slowly kissing on my neck. I grabbed her ass and got a motion going; I repeatedly rubbed it and smacked it occasionally until she moved towards the middle of my body and kissed me down to my clit. She started sucking and snacking on my pussy lips all at the same time, "That shit feel good" I said before I let out a moan. I was trying to control myself, so I sat up and grabbed her head. I pushed her face to sink her lips into the middle of it all; she started fucking me with her tongue. She started moaning, the more she sucked on my clit the more entitled she felt. I laid there enjoying it, fucking her mouth until I was done, and when I nutted, she fingered herself until she was done.

I got up to gather myself for a shower; she was breathing all hard looking more attractive than before. "You satisfied?" I asked her, throwing a towel at her legs. "Very much so." She got up to join me in the shower. I was single but that could change if I met the right guy, and she would have to respect it, period. I also had to make sure she and I were on point first before any of that ever transpired, and find out why she ran off on her last P in the first place. I knew better not to ask because that shit don't concern me, so they say, but in all actuality it does, because knowing a bitch background is just as important.

"How long you been fucking with girls?" I wanted to pick her brain a little bit though. "I've always liked girls, just rare to find one like you." "What you mean like me?" "You're not a stud but you clearly wear the pants all while being pretty and sexy, bitches be either too girly and weak or too manly and ugly." We both started dying laughing. "Thank you babe." "You're welcome, you're so perfect, I swear." She was juicing me hard like bitch, what's the deal? Kill all that. "You funny as fuck. Shit, I'm just me, I'm glad you like it, let's talk about this money though." "Ok I'ma be ready to go in 20 mins." I walked to my closet to throw on some joggers and a Victoria secret hoodie. I couldn't brush my teeth, she was all over the sink with her make-up and hair mess. "So what's your normal program like?" This is ok to ask because if her program been working for her, you don't really want to switch it up unless you worried about the last nigga. "I post online and I just wing it babe, if online not hitting, I'll walk. I don't come home without something, that's a promise." "Ok that's cool; we can see how it go tonight and switch it up some tomorrow." "Ok babe." She seemed to be pretty comfortable, so it didn't really matter if I switched her shit up. "You never thought about dancing?" "Yea, I just made 21 though, so I had to wait." "Oh, ok. Makes sense. Send me all your login info, I'ma screen all yo calls and change some shit up where I see necessary." I had to throw the extras in there so I could fully get in her mix. I need to see her traffic flow and show her why she even paying me in the first place. You can define pimping many ways but it's really all about how you look at it, and how you present it. If she got it all figured out and can do everything herself, what am I here for then? Exactly, either you a lame nigga and you in the way while she trynna build you up, or you bringing shit to the table and building her up, that's what the fuck I'm here for. Pimps work too, Don't get it confused. "Ok babe, cool. Whatever you want, I'm down." She had all the best replies. She for sure the definition of a lil baby that's gon listen. We didn't waste no time, we was out by 11:30 p.m. She grabbed her first date as my bitch by 11:37 p.m. Soon as she hopped out my car, she got a date and broke the nigga for $3 easy. I had to create her a second account to increase the call flow, and let her start back up answering calls for one account. Both accounts were booming, calls coming to my phone and her phone back to back. I told her to text me everything. "When you book a date, where it's at, when you arrive, when you out, and if you passed, plus why." She ain't pass up on nothing though she wasn't playing about our money. All her dates paid $200 or better, she might have booked for $100 but didn't leave that room until she got $200 or better. She was good at that part but she didn't have any regulars. She was too busy, she really didn't need any, but it makes things smoother. Her phone was unorganized; she couldn't remember names and rarely got the same guy twice because she had so many calling at a time. I was about to change all of that and put some structure on her. The next day was when I really bossed her life up. "You need some regulars, blood." "I know, I just be focused on making them nut, I don't be tripping." "Well, this shit be real smooth if you had regulars. Less strain, save money on posting a lot of shit, that come with having regulars so focus on that now." "But how do I even do that babe? I don't really talk to them, I just smile, I mean I never really wanted them to get to know me." My bitch really exotic but would submit herself and they loved it. "Don't trip, I got it. I'ma get it started for you, then you just follow my lead." I started going through her phone texting tricks 1 by 1, if they had ever messaged a room number or anything that was obvious to a finished date. I sent them a message saying, "hey babe" and waited for response. I got a quick 80 replies, and some were asking "who's this?" So, I started sending each guy 1 picture and texted, "thinking about you." The first guy to reply said he had been thinking about Sasha all week and wanted to arrange another visit. I ended up getting Sash a new phone when we added the second account to her profiles, so she was working on that and we would just rotate them throughout the week. She would take some down time and could read my messages and catch up, and get an understanding on how to build up regulars. The first guy I wanted to lock it in with was perfect; he kept texting all night. I went to bed leaving his last text unread but the next morning, I woke up to five messages from him saying basically he needed my bitch to come to LA this week, all on him. She had other messages and most of the guys lived in LA but had gone to Vegas to work for a few days, but now on their way back home. "What's up boo, you tired yet?" I asked, watching Sash undress getting ready to shower her day away. "No, I'm good. You want me?" She was smiling and blushing trying to be sexy, just a straight freak, but all that sex shit was out the door for me until my money got right. "Naw, I don't want you, I got you already and we got shit to do. Get dressed." She pouted her lips and sank her head down, I started laughing and snatched her arm pulling her over to me. "Get yo stanking ass in the shower blood, you know I want you." I leaned in for a kiss slowly and softly. I kissed and nipped at her neck, she smiled, and it was that simple... she was good. I kissed this bitch thinking about if she be kissing these niggas, then we had a talk she broke it down for me. Let me know she wasn't kissing or sucking dick her hoing didn't consist of that and I believed her. I put my trust in her same way she did me but was my pimping compromised? I bent the rules but shit this my game, ima play it my way.

The next day I got us up bright and early. "Where we going?" "To LA, pack you some sexy shit" I said, and within a few hours, we were gone on the next flight to Los Angeles. I got us a nice Airbnb for the week, we needed a good run, a good few days to get this shit really in motion. I had decided right there and then to make this work, to find a way after way no matter the outcome, to never give up until I mastered being a pimp. I belonged to this game, this shit chose me.

Chapter 6

It's in Me, Not on Me

For the first 2 months it was just me and Sash. She wasn't friendly at all, so it surprised me when she brung a bitch home one day. "Babe, this is Mia, she fucking with the team." I didn't like how she said that, hella tacky with it, and that decision was to be made by me. "I'll be the one to decide that, what's up Mia? How was your night?" I asked. "I had a pretty decent night, and I'm even better than before now." She was good, charming like a muthafucka. I couldn't help but laugh, and Sasha looked at me with her big ass eyes, all cute and shit, waiting for my approval. She knew me well enough to know I was fucking with it. "Y'all funny as fuck but umm, show me what yo night looked like." She opened up her bag and broke me off. I sat down to count it all up. When I finished, I looked up at Sash. "That's a cool little night, make yourself comfortable Mia." I had just checked $15,000 out a bitch and my fee was totally going up now. I couldn't help but feel super proud of my bitch, she sure knew how to pick 'em. "Let's celebrate, grab some champagne, there is some rose in the fridge. "Sash, grab the bottle babe, and pour everybody a glass." She did just as I said. "I want us to get in the Jacuzzi and relax tonight." It was still early and I had a good feeling about the team I was building I had to reward them, plus me and Sasha would like to have some fun with Ms. Mia.

We all got into the Jacuzzi and I didn't waste no time. I gently pulled Mia over towards me by her bikini straps and positioned her right in front of me. "Let me check you out real quick, Miss Miaaaaa." She was happy to come and looked good as hell while I started asking her simple questions. We were having a good conversation and getting to know each other, and if she said something I like I would give her more. I started rubbing on her titties while she wrapped her legs around me. I dipped her under the water a few times for fun and we all started laughing. I think that's what really got it going, and I could see how bad both Sash and Mia wanted to play, so I let them play. I watched them, drinking my champagne as they began to rub on each other, Mia started kissing on Sash body down her neck line, careful not to approach her lips. They was giving me a show, they were both warmed up to each other, it was perfect timing. They eventually came over to include me and I was already so turned on and fully ready to feel both of their bodies. Mia got out the pool briefly and went into her bag looking for something, "Sasha, you down?" she held up a small object in her hand; it was a pill. "Yes baby, bring me one, come put it in my mouth," Sash replied. I had never done drugs before and I wasn't about to start. I just watched as they popped a pill to the back of their throats, washing it down with champagne, they were lit within the next 30 minutes, completely naked all on each other for hours, it was like a scene out of a porno, the both of them fighting to get to that climax. I'm thinking to myself, I'm building this bitch, putting her best pieces to her puzzle on display so that she can be great, and as far as sex goes, I gave her full creative control. Let her be free, she was a monster at this. Sash knew me, she knew I wanted her to fuck Mia so good and include me, but without me actually having to do anything. That way she will still long for me, and I was there in the moment touching on her, my breast in her mouth. We wore her out, then I put her in the guest room to get some sleep. The next morning, Mia was up making breakfast, she made herself right at home and had it smelling so good, to my surprise, she could actually cook. When I got Sash, she couldn't cook at all, I had to teach her ass from chicken to rice. "It smells good, what did you make for me?" I asked, kissing Mia on the cheek, grabbing her face at the same time. "I made smothered potatoes." "Damn, that's my favorite." "Eggs, bacon, and waffles." "That sounds so good love. Did you make the waffles on the stove, or in the toaster "on the stove" Sasha must have told her how I like it, "perfect" she was on point and that was cool, but today would be the real test. They had to work tonight and I was eager to see what Mia could produce. "Babe, it's some fruit on the table, also I'm making your plate now. Have a seat, I'll bring it to you." I sat down to relax and eat on the fruit when Mia came over and began to massage my shoulders and back, then she lightly kissed me on my neck repeatedly, over and over again. She went up to my ear, kissing and licking, then she whispered, "Thank you for having me." Sash made her plate, and we all sat down at the table together to eat, as a family, as a team.

Mia had set the standard for me and from that point forward, if the bitch wasn't coming in my door appreciative and sexy, and with the attitude of I bought a bag for you, they could not be a part of my team, let alone speak to me. I was a boss bitch, age 16, building my empire, 20 toes kicking, who's going tell me something?

My girls got ready, hella cute. They didn't do a lot of makeup, just enough to pop. Besides, they both had pretty faces and skin, all they had to keep up with was lashes, eyebrows, and nails. And Sash had plenty of hair enough for all 3 of us, babe just gorgeous. I made sure they had good days leading to great nights. So, I wasn't surprised later that night when Mia and Sash both hit the goal in an hour. One $2000, the other $1800, the money was coming so quick. As long as they both made $1500 a night, they could come in and it didn't matter if it happened in 30 minutes, it was good to come home as long as you had made something. They both were seeing on average about $1200 a night or more. They would hit $800 but still keep working so hard. Mia was exactly how I motivated her to be, she knew the minute to come home but I also knew they weren't out there to bullshit, and I really admired hard work. I wanted to reward them and show them both how much they meant to me, so I started buying them designer things. Sash already had gotten her first Gucci bag after she passed her 90 days. Then I got her some red bottoms right after Mia came. I'm going to start buying them matching items so they could feel equal and know that they are in this shit together. They would get out there looking like twins, matching red bottoms, matching bags, matching tops, they even got matching hair sometimes. My girls were getting all the other hoes' attention and it wasn't a competition, they both were damn good team players. My girls were happy, and it was obvious because eventually, every night they would try to bring a girl home. I repeatedly turned down everything for the first few months. Until Mia was fully locked in, I wouldn't welcome another bitch to our team. This made the other hoes want me even more; they wanted to pay me so bad and you know that I wasn't pressuring no bitch, so if you do come, you gotta come correct. Finally, halfway into May, the girls brung home two new bitches; one each, I called it a double up.

I was coming down the stairs and could hear Sasha say "let me do all of the talking." I had my Versace robe on she had got me for Christmas last year.

When the girls arrived at the guard gate of our community, Sash gave the names of the two new girls. Normally, I would stop everything right at the gate but I let them in today. One girl's name was Ava Smith and the other was Lily Pederson, snow, I came down cracking a joke, "So, it's Lilly Smith and Ava Pederson?" I mixed up their names on purpose to get the ice broken, they all starting to crack up laughing. "No I'm Ava Smith, and this is Lilly," said Ava. "Ohhh, ok cool. It's nice to meet you both, I'm Sid."

I wanted them to relax and not come with the drag. Sash hadn't even been to sleep yet, she'd been working hard all night. "Mia and I wanted to bring them home to meet you, and was thinking maybe we can have some fun... celebrate your birthday a little." You know, she always said that fly shit. Sasha could do no wrong in my eyes, that's my baby for real. I started to smile, then I leaned over to kiss her on the mouth, she was the only bitch I would kiss on, I didn't care about the pimp rules. It was different for me being a female, besides, that's my bitch regardless. "Whatever you want to do is cool love, just get it started." I whispered to her passing by to head back upstairs. I lightly pinched Sasha on her ass and gave Mia a wink to kinda let them know they did a good job, but I was going to give Mia some attention later. "Hey, Mia, grab some champagne." "Ok babe! You guys like champagne right?" she asked the girls "yes," they both replied "Babe loves champagne, that's all we drink, so I'm going to pour everyone a glass and we're going to just chill and get to know you guys."

Lily decided to make a toast, "to this wonderful evening with amazing people, may I have the honor to endure the journey of new levels with this beautiful team." A toast to chasing the bag and living our best lives is what I was thinking at the top of the stairs.

I didn't want to ask about the fee, I wanted to see if these were real hoes or if they were new. I made my way back downstairs "So, what brings you ladies here tonight?" "Babe" "Sash, I'm talking to these two, let them speak." Ava spoke first, "I am here because I see your girls often and I've been trying to get to you for months now. I would like to be a part of your team, if you will have me." She looked at me for a response but I stayed quiet. Lilly spoke, "I'm here because I want this to be my home. I want to pay you." And that right there was a perfect example of getting straight to it. "I've heard great things about a white girl, and Ava you looking good too. I like you both, and I'm considering to move forward, anything else you need to add?" They both pulled out their fee. Ava had $18,000 and Lily had $13,600; neither of them knew my fee or knew what each other had to pay, they just knew that they both had to pay. "Ok cool, we gon chill tonight, have some fun." Sasha knew what that meant, she knew that she was fucking tonight, but it was perfect because I could get some one on one time with Mia. I had been starving her for months and still never even went there with her. I had just moved us to a private condo out the way; it had a pool and gym within the community and a private Jacuzzi for each condo, it wasn't a very hot night so we decided to hang out at the Jacuzzi. I always made the girls get in the jacuzzi crazy as it sounds but them chemicals will clean a bitch quick. Wash all that makeup off I liked to see those faces fully also. With Champagne and pretty girls, this was the perfect combination. "Come here Mia." I pulled her in with my legs then wrapped them around her tight, and she started rubbing on my ass and trying to suck on my boobs. I could tell her pussy was throbbing just from standing next to me, she would tell me how intrigued she was by me and how bad she wanted to taste me. I just knew she would make sure I enjoyed it. The other girls watched as I leaned my head back and closed my eyes as she lifted me up out of the water and set me on the rim. "Can I pull you closer? Can I kiss on your thighs?" She asked. "Sasha turn on some music." "Ok babe, what you feel like hearing? One of y'all got a playlist?" I could tell she wanted to come over and join in or even remove me, but she was in pocket, otherwise gon get her little feelings hurt. She logged into the Wi-Fi and asked Alexa to play a song "Alexa, play Troy Ave, she belongs to the game" they all began dancing and singing along to the song. Mia poured more champagne and the girls had already been drinking earlier, so now they were super loaded. Ava took off her top and started dancing with her cute ass. She got back in the water and tried to kiss Sasha, Sash pulled back and had her kiss Lily. She knew I'll beat that ass, we don't kiss these hoes. She brung Lilly in so she wasn't looking

119

excluded and boom, they started up a threesome. Meanwhile Mia and I slipped away without them noticing us. I took Mia back inside to have sex for the first time. Her pussy was so warm and tight, she was guiding my hand around her body to show me where she liked to be touched, that's when she leaned in for a kiss but I politely kissed her cheek, then her neck, leading to her tits. She started to moan. "I want you so bad" she quickly flipped me over pulling my panties off to play with my vagina, separating my lips and saying, "All this chocolate, I knew it was pink in the inside." She was turning me on so sexy with her demeanor, and soon she started smacking on my pussy using her whole mouth. I was trying hard not to cum because I wanted to see what she was able to do next. She sat her pussy directly on top of mine and started scissoring them together. I said, "You like it baby." She was gently grinding, sucking on my titties. She took her finger and gently went inside of me with a little motion she had going; she was comfortable as fuck. I was thinking how she knew how to do this shit so well, but it didn't even matter. That shit felt so great but once I figured out her motion, I lifted her up in the air and laid her on her back. "I'm getting on top now" I said, because I was in control of this shit "this my shit, you my bitch."

That's how we ended our night good vibes, hella money being made.

"This bitch Lilly ain't even passed her 90 days without fucking up and now she just gotta go, plain and simple; I'm done, she's fired." I was on the phone with my friend, talking to him because one of his bitches at the time was Lilly's sister. "She a goer but you gotta watch her Sid, gotta be down that bitch throat with it, and you can't slip up or she will." At the time he said it I didn't know what he meant, but my point of calling him up on that day was to laugh and let him know I get it now. "Why didn't you just tell me, bro?" I asked. "Aye, now you know people be sensitive about snow, I'm just saying I ain't want to be the one to tell you." This bitch had serious issues like separation type shit, eating disorders, she a liar and top it off, the bitch on drugs. He continued to talk, "It took me a year to clean her sister up but that's on you if you want to make that type of commitment." "I don't think I want to, I'm cool. I'll have to pass, it's too much work," I replied. "Only reason I did it with sis is because I was hurting; she was my first bitch, my only bitch and I was just jumping in the game not knowing shit, so I had to go hard or go home." "Ain't no buts bro, if two bitches on drugs, both are hoes, both out here lost in these streets, they are equal because it don't matter at this point if you do just a little drugs or a lot, you still a drug user, and an unstable hoe." We both started laughing. "Seriously though, I gave this bitch so many chances I'm all out, got no more time to waste and if you want her, come get her." "Naw, I'm good. I can't do nothing with that. Already got my hands full, I'll hit you right back though." We hung up laughing, this shit was funny but annoying. I remember my brother saying all money is not good money, do not just allow anything because that is when shit falls apart. I ran downstairs to Lilly, she was lounging on the couch pretending to be woke. "Get yo high ass up and go pack yo shit, you gotta go." "But why babe, where am I going? Please don't make me leave." I was prepared for her to freak out, and I wasn't having it at all. "I'm not high babe just a little tired; I've been working hard, you said so yourself." "Lilly, listen, you lying to me makes this situation no better. How can you just lie like this?" "I'm sorry, I don't want you upset with me I just got a little bit high I didn't do too much, I swear." "Well look, that's cool or whatever but you can't kick the drugs so you can't stay here. You no good for this team so I need you to go." "I made more money last night, I can give it to you." "I don't want your money, what don't you understand?" "But baby, I will die for this team." That was the problem right there, nobody wanted her to die for us, we wanted to get to this bag. She was crying like a 5-year-old with a face full of snot. "I'm sending you to rehab, you gotta clean up. I'm not fucking with no meth head!" This bitch jumped up out her seat and plunged herself at me with her hands clawed "Argggghhh." "Bitch what the fuck are you doing? See this that weird shit. You're done, you need help for real." "I'm not high, I'm not, I swear." "Alright bitch, I'm about to drug test you and if you high, I'm finna beat yo ass, period, for even playing with me." I never said that to none of my girls before, but I was tired of Lilly. I finally got Lilly out the house and to rehab; I used the money she had made the last month to pay for her stay of a minimum of 16 months. I stayed in constant contact with her throughout her entire stay. I wrote letters, went to visit when I had time, and sent pictures for her to reminisce. My home boy who had dealt with this similar drug problem with Lilly's sister had gone about it wrong. He kept giving her the drugs until it was almost too late, and that's what made her kick the shit, but not Lilly; she hasn't had a scared straight moment yet, all she knew was the feeling of being high. "I live in the real world; I hate it here. So, I get high to excuse myself and drown out the pain." Lilly would tell us this all the time and we would just lightly laugh, but she was really feeling something and tried numerous times to express herself; you can't ignore the signs of suicidal behavior. After she completed rehab, she came back better than before. "You look like you gained a little weight." I said. I was picking her up from her last rehab meeting. "I've gained about 40 babe, do I look good?" "Yes, you look healthy and happy." She had gained in all the right places and got some color too. "Babe I brung everybody a gift, is that ok?" She was the sweetest person you'll ever meet. "Yea that's cool, what you got us?" She pulled out some DIY bracelets she had made at the rehabilitation center. "Aww, how sweet of you Lilly." We all were smiling at each other; happy to get gifts. "Ok but I'm not done, I got one more gift ladies!" She pulled out a bottle of rose. "Bitchhhh yesss, you read my mind." Sasha shouted, "Ok, I want to make a toast, grab us all a glass somebody, while I pop this baby open." "Welcome home Lil, I really missed you and that ass too girl; it grew, ok!" Mia hit Lilly on her ass. "Oh yes, you looking real fly Lil," Ava added as she reached her glass towards Lilly to pour her up some champagne. We all then raised our glasses while Lily made a toast. "I'm toasting to someone caring enough about my well-being, because when I wasn't strong enough to care for me, you guys did. I'm toasting to second chances and I'm toasting to my muthafucking team dog!" "Eyyyy! Ok! Gang in here." Mia was juicing everybody trying to get shit fired up. I felt real good, honestly, I thought I lost one but because I was understating to her upbringing, I never passed any judgment I just provided her with the help I felt she needed, and now look. I invested in my bitch, I built her back up. "Lilly come here love." She was across the room getting ready to take her clothes off. "Yes babe?" "I'm proud of you and I'm glad you're back; stay on track and let's run this money up!" I kissed her on her forehead, she smiled and walked away with her eyes on me; I could tell she was proud of herself and no longer in a dark place.

Chapter 7

At All Cost

I t's been hectic trying to maintain but all my bitches are a reflection of me, and they have my same work ethic. These girls were hoeing daily, but they weren't the only ones bringing home money every night. I didn't become a hoe, but I did become a Madame, a female pimp and let's not forget, an escort on occasions and even a masseuse. I did it all; anything to try and build up clientele for my team and our next move. I had a clear vision, so I wasn't wasting no money, wasn't hustling backwards, none of that. People knew of me, but I stayed off the scene because niggas just assumed they could knock me and get this whole million dollar package. To their surprise, none of these niggas in the game knew me and that's because I be on bitches and I'm real discreet with it. My girls did the networking with other hoes and would test bitches considering to leave home, so the nigga just always assumed I was a nigga, and he also assumed my bitch was curious about his home.

I had a new bitch waiting on my porch almost every day. "What's up love, can I help you?" I asked this blonde headed chick sitting on my porch looking like she was defeated. "Yes, I got a home girl here, she said. I could come fuck with y'all; can you bring me inside and introduce me, please? She's not answering." "Sure love, get up and come inside. Take your shoes off at the door too." We stepped in and I asked her to have a seat. My plan was to just keep talking to her, ask a few questions, see how she interacts with me, and see if she's got a temper. "Alright, so tell me about yourself." "Ok... well, after getting chased by the guards at the gate, I first thought this is dumb, you're not going to even give me a chance after knowing I snuck in, but then I thought maybe you would see that I was determined and eager, and that's what I can tell you about me. I'm not here to play, I'm not lazy. I promise, I'ma get up and chase the bag daily." That was dope to me that she snuck in and almost got caught, and was funny as hell. "It's all good, we gon check it out, get to know each other, and if we mesh, well then, hey we moving forward." "Aw babe, really? You're so bomb, I swear I won't disappoint you."

I was officially five bitches deep. My new bitch Katie, is cool as hell. Now it's time to switch up my program, see hoeing gets old just as dancing gets old, you think these bitches want to die a hoe? As dumb as you might think a hoe is, they are actually normal people with goals and dreams too. I knew all my hoes on a personal level and knew what they had dreams of becoming, dreams of places they wanted to go, things they wanted to do, and it was my job to get them to the top.

My brother used to always tell me not to talk that school shit around his bitches, because they will start to think they can go off to college, become more than a hoe; he said that's all they were meant to be and all they would ever be. That wasn't smart to me; I felt the opposite about it when the time came, and I had five bitches of my own now. I started thinking to myself how I should have all my bitches taking some kinda online course or something. I wanted them to be smart as I am or even smarter, especially if they're loyal to me.

"Alright y'all, everybody come check it out real quick, team meeting," I yelled out to the girls, gathering them all in the living room. "What's up dad, everything good?" Ava asked. "Yup, all good. I got some new shit I want us to play around with." "Ok, what's up babe? We all here," said Sasha. "So, I started this group chat online with a few gentlemen I know; most of them are older men and all of them are very well paid married men." "Ok, and they want to book us?" "Nope, they aren't looking for sex, just massages, so we gon play it like the real clubs do in Vegas. No sex, and we can accept tips too. I'm going to check out a few spots today and update everybody, but we starting this weekend for sure." "I'm ready, this gon be fun." "Exactly, it's gon be easy, real chill. Y'all gon wear something sexy, everybody matching. It's gon be wine and snacks, and other entertainment. The guy can inform the host of whichever girl he wants to book, and she will take him to the back for a massage with a happy ending." I didn't mention the part about them taking the dealer classes yet ha, I'm not sure how they would feel but in order to do these we gotta back it with some documents . "I love it babe! Yes, this is so dope." Sasha was excited. "Cool, I'm glad you feeling it. I got my boy to make you guys all certified masseuses I want you to get dressed and go buy everybody's uniform. We finna run it up with this. Aye, y'all got jobs now, let's see who can do both."

It was time for me to manipulate the game. I was taking everything from my brother. All the shit I saw him fuck up at I flipped into a better situation, and all of his accomplishments, I kept the same routine but took it even further with a better outlook. I wanted to do what he wasn't able to do because the money blinded him, but more importantly, I wanted to bring my vision to life; together we woulda killed it. He was so good, but he only had a one track mind which was his downfall. My bitches were no longer just some regular hoes, they were smart. I kept my word, we moved to L.A and I had them all enrolled into two units of communications class. They could now think for themselves in my absence; they could articulate very well, and hold educated conversations. I needed them to feel relatable and confident in themselves, so I sent them on missions to new places, learning new sports, and finding new clientele. "Baby, we branched out!" Ava said to a girl she met at a bar earlier, and we were now interviewing her for a real job. We needed to hire some regular girls to stand at the door of our 2nd location "Well Kept" wine club. We had partnered with a man at the first location in Oakland but now, the Vegas location was all ours and we needed a hostess. Her job description would be to greet for four hours and off before the second half of the club got started. This was just in case some shit ever went down you know, the police show up or whatever could possibly occur we was ready, and this was a legit wine club for gentlemen only. I had thought this through fully and was getting all my licenses that same week on top of a permit. It was my first business endeavor, my baby and I were proud of myself. My ambition came from having nothing, then it came from the idea of losing it all once I got it. I had also watched my brother lose. He didn't have a good program in place, they didn't know how to work without him, let alone maintain. He would be frustrated as hell and say shit like, "I'm back at ground zero, this shit ain't possible no more." He was defeated at times, but every time he managed to get back up and get it going, yet it was at a standstill once he reached his peak, he ain't know how to level up no more, no more than he had already done before. To top it off, they were all getting old. I'd sit back and watch it get chaotic and my heart would hurt for my brother so I did what any sister would do. I peeked my head in his room and said, "At least you on the ground, may be at zero but pick up yo head and start running bro." He would laugh and call me all type of squares, and tell me, "Get out yo feelings." Ha, but it would work, he would literally get his ass up and go. That's what made him start saying, "Say some fly shit, sis," because of this right here, he would tell me that it wasn't even me talking. "Them not even yo words though, punk! That's momma talking." I loved the idea of that and began to believe it in my heart, she talking through me, always giving me the words to say.

"Watch over me momma, I love you, I miss you."

Our new business was booming; it was safe, less risk involved, and the girls had fun on top of no longer having to fuck for the money. I mean, they still did what they had to do, and because the guys of the club had no idea that the ladies giving massages were mine, they would often try to ask for outside services or book a girl for their own private event.

I could easily have kicked them out the club. I mean, my girls tell me immediately but instead, I just run their information and if nothing comes up, I would sick the girls on him and they would find a way to get in his wallet. "Don't stop looking till you find something." A few times we had guys who were cops, we got them good but they legit real members now, and just warn me every now and then to slow up with the ads. The first cop had a real ID; we ran his name, got his info, and went back over to the room where Ava was sucking the soul out of his dick and presented him with it. "So, look, we know you're a cop, but it's all good, we ain't tripping if you ain't tripping, you tripping?" "Tripping? Umm I don't think so, I'm just here for a massage, sorry if I offended anyone." He was so nervous, that's the cool thing about Vegas, you network with all kinds of people. I knew he wasn't gon bust a move though, just had a feeling everything was good. "Alright cool, well I had to make sure and also before I go, I do have you recorded here just for our personal records. We hope to see you again now that we have this cleared up."

He was giving me a look that could kill but shit, I had to protect my business by any means. The cops knew not to play with me at all. I mean, I wasn't untouchable, but majority of the Las Vegas officers were on tape getting sucked by Ava or Lilly.

My girls were happy, but they were ready to get back on the scene; it had been a few months of us consistent with the club, just work no play and these girls were ready. "I wanna get so turnt up and pop hella bottles on bitches' booties all night." Sasha was such a freak, I was surprised that was all that came out her mouth. "I wanna throw some ones on a bitch and get hella lap dances, I bet they still can't do it better than me." Mia always got us into something whenever we stepped out and this is why.

I kinda wanted to get lit and enjoy my night somewhere too, I started thinking about how I just barely turned 17 and wasn't really comfortable on the adult scene yet. I mean, I had a fake ID, so it wasn't an issue, I just couldn't wait till I was legit. I'm not sure why I didn't really want to go to the club exactly, maybe I was scared to lose a bitch or scared to step on the scene. I just wasn't sure what type of night I'd be walking into if I ran into someone I knew.

"Dad, Migos will be at Drais tonight, let's go." "Ava, Migos is always there, that ain't nothing new. I want to do some different shit." I could tell I threw her off when I said that, but she just switched sides and rode my clit like a real one is supposed to. "Me too dad, I'm actually tired of Drais I used to always go, but I'm down for whatever." This Bitch been with me a good eight months, she ain't went to Drais not once, so I'm not sure what she talking about. "Alright I'll take you guys somewhere tonight, it should be cool, just chill out."

I gathered my thoughts and started making plans for us to get some type of excitement going.

A few hours later, we arrived at the surprise spot I wanted to take them to. "What the fuck is this place?" Sasha asked as we pulled over to park; she was driving one car and Mia followed behind in her car. "Just park Sash, trust me it's cool."

We had arrived to this Moroccan style restaurant; the outside looked like a hole in the wall, but I had been there before and the food was bomb. "I'm not about to go in here babe, I'm sorry ugh fail." Sasha was cutting up and once she started, they all got started. "Yea dad, what she said. I mean, look at this place, why did I even bother getting dressed?" "You bitches are being hella typical right now just shut the fuck up and get out my car."

The place was just as I remembered it, with well lit up low tables, with floor pillows used for seats but there was also both style seats for when the dancers came out. We ordered our food and shortly after, the dancers came out. It was very similar to the strip club. One by one, they did individual dances pulling their tops off halfway through the song and re-dressing before the second song ended. The first dancer was gorgeous; she interacted with the crowd for a little bit then she spotted Lilly and insisted on pulling her up from the floor to teach her some belly dance moves. Lilly got the hang of it quick and soon after, another dancer came out. They were all over Lilly like they never seen snow before. She was following the belly dancers' moves step by step trying to get the hang of it, and more dancers came out to give the rest of us lap dances but there wasn't a dancer for Mia; she was cracking up laughing, watching everyone until a dancer came out just for her. She had on very few bells around her waist and had a bottle of oil. She grabbed Mia's hands and poured the oil in her palms, making it over flow down her arms and she lead her hands to her booty, positioning Mia to massage and caress it. they all joined in and did the same; poured oil in their hands and began to massage the dancer's body. "This feels so good ladies." The dancer was loving it, she looked like she was about to explode and my girls were ready to eat her apart, literally. About 20 minutes later, she kissed them on the cheek saying thank you a million times and finally disappeared into the back of the room. "Babe, I'm feeling this place, think this gon be our new spot." Sasha was too cute when she was excited, I knew they would like it. My real reason for coming was to talk business to the owner and try to get Sasha working the floor there regularly. If I got her dancing here, she could short stop so much shit. I wanted us to start one of our own more up to date, so I had already prepped her on how to observe and take notes on shit, mental notes. I wanted to own a massage/gentlemen's club, plus this style of Moroccan club full of beautiful women, and there was one more goal on my list. I was working so hard building our brand on most days, I forgot to take care of me. Things were on the up, but I was beyond stressed out trying to finish all of my projects. I wasn't getting any sleep and I wasn't eating like I should have. I was trying to eat financially and although I was focused, I was starting to question myself and wonder if I had let the emotions of these women and this fast lifestyle get to me. This shit was like having three full-time jobs working 40 hours a week on top of three dogs, man, I was exhausted. From one bitch crying about helping her mother pay some bills, to another bitch just straight bitching she wanted her own car, it was too much some days. No matter what was going on though, I'd turn to look at Sasha, and she was my release to it. I swear to God, she wasn't asking for shit, she wasn't complaining, and she stayed out my way. "Babe, how are you feeling today, are you ok?" She asked me this daily. I knew she was concerned about my mental health, and that I was a priority in her life. I had to step my bitch up even more now. She deserved it fully, and I was about to do it for her, long as she stayed down.

Chapter 8

Mentally Drained

The thought of having sex to make money was very appealing to so many women, you'd be surprised to know how many actually enjoyed it versus the ones who had no choice. I was getting inquiries left and right, but my team had retired from hoeing; briefly and they were now escorts. My girls only dealt with routine clients for referrals. Hoeing was so hot anyway, and if anyone went to jail too many times accumulating a real record, she then becomes no good to me. I needed bitches with good credit and no records for the type of shit I was on. I needed ladies who were assets otherwise I didn't need them at all and that's what made my pimping different. We had leveled up so much that we even had an office with a receptionist who booked each girl for the entire month, according to their availability. We were officially pros, legit all around for the most part, and it was cool, but I kept feeling like why stop there? I had a million ideas draining me out because all I could focus on was being a pimp. I'd been exposed to the lifestyle so young that my mentality and thought process was much different from others. At first, I would cry myself to sleep being reminded of the mental abuse I experienced and the manipulative home and structured family I had. I didn't have time for school because I had lied about my age and created this whole persona to my Team. It was too late to go back now, besides what did I need a high school diploma for? I wanted to go to a prom, I really did and what about a senior trip. I didn't have time to grow up officially. The money grew me up quickly.

My dad was in fact a pimp, but he was different with me maybe because I was his baby girl. He spoke soft and never lied. My brother was the same way with me at first, loving and gentle, and you better not had fucked with me. He would come in a hurry, but after auntie Tanya died, things started to change. D.J had to step up and I believe he did so the best way he knew how. He became intimidating, in your face with it, mean and often annoyed. He was so angry about his childhood so he found ways to take it out on the people he loved. I knew he loved me, but that wasn't enough because right next to that thin line of love, there was a even thinner line of hate to be crossed. I woke up one day and he hated me, literally and there was no doubt about it. I was trying to make him proud, but the thing was he wasn't even proud of who he had become. I was mentally abused by my brother day in and day out. I had become such a burden to him, and his mouth was uncontrollable. The things he would say started to really get to me, and being an ugly African American bitch had bothered me to the point of no return.

I felt like I wasn't pretty enough to be a hoe because if my brother thought I was dark skinned and ugly, I was certain the world viewed me as such, or like I didn't qualify. I remember feeling like nothing I did would ever be good enough, so instead he locked me away in a back room ashamed of me. Or was this a figment of my imagination? Was I actually in the front room full of confusion? I was in the mix of it all, trying to hold on to my innocence. I fumbled through the medicine cabinet and found some pills one day thinking I should just kill myself, who would miss me anyway? I went downstairs to get a glass of water filled to the brim. "Yo boyfriend called," D.J said to me as I walked by. He was referring to a guy from the hood I started to sorta deal with, until I found out him and my bro were somewhat friends. So, that was another thing added to the list of reasons to fuck with me. I swear, D.J wanted me to be gay or something, super tough or something, because he kinda treated me like the son he never had. "Who cares?" I replied, then I decided to take the pills right there in the kitchen in front of everybody. I was tired of my life being put on public display like everybody was perfect and I wasn't, like it was fair for these bitches to have an excuse such as daddy issues to do the things they did and act the way they acted, but there I was. No damn daddy and no fucking sympathy, let along an excuse, on top of having to deal with a person who sometimes came off as a narcissist but later on values my opinion. The shit was a total bi-polar rollercoaster, which I could never get off of. I was daydreaming, replaying my past life over and over like a sad movie.

"What you doing? Go back upstairs now." D tried to shoo me away; I leaned my head back and dropped 20 pills down my throat, quickly swallowing the water behind "fuck you" I whispered trying not to cry any more of my tears for this heartless man. "Bitch is you dumb? Aye Jas, get her. she just swallowed some pills, she gon pass out." I definitely didn't want to die, though as afraid of death as I was, I knew I just wanted to stir things up around there and I did just that. Someone called the cops and all type of case workers were ar the house an on his ass. Guess who started to feel bad, stupid ass me. I understood the fact that we both had not been raised right, then I started to break shit down. Ok, in life you're either a pimp or a hoe. Why would he be a hoe, cuz he light skinned and light skinned niggas be hoes! Or like they say, dark skinned bitches be ugly. The stereotypes were so typical and depressing, but that's when I decided I wasn't no black ugly bitch either, and I also wasn't gonna be broke. I for damn sure wasn't settling for stupid. All the names he called me, all the words he felt like I represented were wrong.

The next day I woke up in the hospital surrounded by bitches. "Now you bitches care, huh?" I couldn't believe it. These hoes were sobbing all over me, and believe it or not, they were all little girls dying inside just like me. "The doctor had to pump the pills out of you. They caught it just in time sis, those were narcos." I didn't even know what a narco was, thank God they got me here. I started to cry, laying in the bed thinking about that dumb ass shit I just tried to do.

The doctor came to my aid and began to ask me a million questions. "Are you suffering from depression? Was this your first time having suicidal thoughts?" "Yes, I'm depressed, I miss my mom and dad, and my brother. Please let me go home." I got released a few days later. After tests and counseling, they finally felt comfortable enough to let me leave. I just knew I was going to John George or somewhere for crazy people. When I got home, my brother was there and to my surprise, he was nice to me. Of course, he's never going to say sorry, but he did greet me and made sure my room was clean and I was comfortable, and for that, I am forever grateful. I continued off to my room. There I sat silent in the dark and when I almost wanted to pray, I stopped because I knew God wouldn't give me none of the things I was about to cry out for. My mom was gone and no matter how bad I wanted her or needed her, she was never coming back. It took me about a week to shake myself out of whatever it was I was going through. I mean, I was ok, but I couldn't eat and I didn't want to leave my room. At first, I was embarrassed, then I just became lazy and ungrateful literally, too lazy to get out of bed until my brother stopped having everybody bring me food. I'm not sure if it was him who made sure there was a plate pushed to the side for me, forcing me to get out of bed and eat, or if it was someone else. Whomever it was I appreciated, because at this point, I had no desire to even fight.

"Sidney, you ok babe?" Sash had walked in on me crying. "Yea, I'm just daydreaming about some shit from my past. I'm cool though." I was having more and more flashbacks of my life like I was being haunted. Or did I just miss them, missing my brother. I hadn't heard or seen him in a year. Since leaving the house that day, I got so focused. All I did all day every day was make money, it was the only way to stay busy, and staying busy blocked the painful memories. Was I living life or stressing life? I got to the point where I started to become lonely, I had everything... a business, money and bitches, but something was missing.

"I'm headed out, y'all don't wait up for me. I gotta take care of some stuff alone." I started going out on my own; I wasn't doing shit, just stuff like going to catch a movie, even reading a book at the park. I would catch regular flights back and forth to Oakland. I could feel my mental health slipping, so I just started doing things to make me feel good. It felt good being in Oakland but apart of me wanted to really get a away, let it go for good.

"I've been seeing you out here a lot lately, you from around here?" "Who? Me?" Some random guy just started talking to me one day while I was tucked off at some park in the dubs trying to read this last chapter. "Yea you, ain't nobody else around here." He started laughing and walking off probably thinking to himself, this bitch crazy. "Wait! My bad. I'm Sidney and I'm not from over here, but I be around." I said secretly. "That's cool, well nice to meet you Sid, I'm K.C." he extends his hand to shake mine, but I stood up and replied "K.C? Wow, I remember you from the party some years back." "Hell yea, I remember that was you, look at you though, all grown up and shit." I was supposed to catch a flight to L.A the next day but after running into dude

146

I canceled and reserved me a room for the week hey, might as well enjoy myself.

That next day, I returned to the park at the same time hoping K.C would show up again, but he didn't. Ok, this was so stupid waiting around for some nigga, what is wrong with me? I left and ended up down the street on Mac Arthur ordering a fat ass burger from ½ burger joint, and that's when he saw me.

I was standing outside ordering my food when he pulled into the parking lot. "Excuse me, can I talk to you for a minute?" Poking his head out the window he was trying to get my attention; I never even turned his way. Luckily for me, K.C walked up behind me. "Can you add a bacon burger with everything on it, cheese too and fries to that?" Standing behind me, he reached and handed the lady a $20 bill paying for my food as well. "Turn around and give me a hug, you look like you having a bad day." I did as he said and immediately felt better; we started walking towards his car. "So, what's up? You got some time for me today?" He was in a Benz truck this time and someone was in the back seat. "Yes I do. I mean, I got a little bit of time." "Ok cool. You wanna leave yo car here and just ride and chill with me for a min?" "Yea that's cool." "Get in the front, I'ma grab our food." I got in and the girl sitting in the back said hi, and that was it. I immediately knew he was a P, but what I didn't know was what his intentions for me were.

He dropped the chick off on the blade, and he slowly circled through to keep an eye on her. He did it effortlessly, trying to maintain my attention, he let me get to know him some more. I hated the fact that he was a pimp, but there was much more to him than that. He sold drugs too, I wasn't sure what kind yet, but his traffic flow was heavy, he had people meeting him on every corner in that area. What intrigued me was when he got out the car, about six credit cards fell out his pocket right into his seat.

When he closed the door, I picked up a few to read the name. It was some Muslim name I couldn't even pronounce, was that his real name? This guy was so mysterious, so different, I had been waiting for a nigga like him to come my way. I stayed with him the whole day and when he finally drove me to my room, I couldn't help myself and invited him up. "You wanna come up for a little bit, you look exhausted, you can rest some if you want?" I didn't know his living situation but if he was anything like me, a break from home was exactly what he needed. "Man hell yea, you sure?" "Yea, it's good it's just me here." He smiled. I could tell that meant thank you. He grabbed a duffel bag from his trunk and a Louis Vuitton backpack from his back seat. We got to the room and he put up the do-not disturb sign then locked the door behind him. "I'm finna hit this water real quick, cool?" "Ok, I'll go after you." He had his shower gels and cologne and shaving case, that shit is such a turn on, I couldn't help myself. I went straight to the bathroom, took my clothes off and got in with him. "I was waiting for yo thick ass," he said, smiling so hard I could see all his teeth. He grabbed my body and hugged me from the back. "You everything, I promise," he whispered but instead of fucking me, he washed me up. I was cracking up in my head like, okayyy this nigga said naw bitch fuck that, you gotta clean the fuck up first. I'm so extra goofy, he was just real chill like me, and funny because I'm not thick at all. He was like a male version of me, no press and that made me want it even more. My phone was going off like crazy. Sasha was starting to worry about me; I had been gone for a few days now and to separate myself from my own reality, I had my phone on do not disturb mode. "So, what we doing?" K.C was begging for my attention. "Ok I'm getting up today, promise." "Unless you just some type of baller you ain't got no work to do, then let me know shit." He was getting suspicious of me because I was too comfortable. I washed up quickly and got dressed. "Let me take you somewhere today, a few places I love in the bay." "Alright let's go." I started off with breakfast at the Montclair Egg Shop. "You like mimosas?" "Yup yup." "Ok let me get two pomegranate mimosas," I said to the waitress. "This a chill spot, how you find this?" K.C asked me "Oh, I was over here one day and just wondered inside." I couldn't help but notice his phone going off with calls and texts, so I said something. "You good over there?" "Yea this bitch keeps blowing me up, I'ma hit her in a second though, ain't nothing to worry about." I definitely had nothing to worry about, we were barely dating and if a chick thought she was gon come to me, I was gon let her ass know straight up. I'm guessing this girl had a location on him because she came right into the egg shop and pulled up a seat. Lucky for her, this place was really classy and family friendly otherwise I woulda gone there but instead, I kicked back and let K.C handle it. "What's up Noona?

What you doing here? I told you I was eating breakfast with a friend and now you being rude." He was so calm and sexy "I know, I know, I'm sorry but I called you a million times. This couldn't wait bae." I wasn't sure who this girl was, but he excused himself and stepped outside. I packed our food to go and paid for it, prepared to help him if needed. I stepped outside to hear the girl crying "I walked in on him, she only 10 and she was enjoying it so I didn't know what else to do, I recorded them then I left." "What Shay don't believe you?" "She kicked me out, saying I'm judging her nigga. I never liked him, I don't know what to do." "Send her dumb ass the video. Alright look, stop tripping. You just gotta run it up and get you a spot, I got you." This girl had three suitcases with her, she had got an Uber with her whole life packed in them suitcases. "What's up K? What she need? Anything I can do to help?" I whispered to him looking at the girl crying. "She just finally ready to get some money, you know anything about that?" "Yea I know some shit, I got you." That was our first project together; we had to build her back up from ground zero. K said she been ready to pay him but she was just too much of a headache, he would shake her any chance he could but if I could put good use to her and deal with her accordingly, then he was down. "I'm down for whatever you down for, babe." I was excited to show him what I was capable of, but I wasn't ready to fully expose myself. He was looking at me like he wanted to eat me up. We got K a room near the blade and parted ways, with plans to put her to work later on.

K.C and I wanted to finish our day off the way we planned but we ended up chillin in his car talking for hours. "Never met a you before, baby where did you come from?" He asked "I came from nothing, grew up right here out on these east Oakland streets." He didn't say anything to my reply, he just looked at me. So I continued "I don't know much about my dad, but my mom was killed when I was six and my dad disappeared." "I'm sorry to hear that love, that type of story either make you or break you." He was right, but I wasn't sure if it was breaking me or making me. "I'm at a point where I really want to find my dad, I think I just need some closure."

Chapter 9

Dad, What Part of the Game is This!?

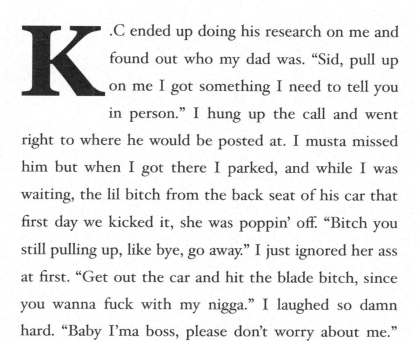

K.C ended up doing his research on me and found out who my dad was. "Sid, pull up on me I got something I need to tell you in person." I hung up the call and went right to where he would be posted at. I musta missed him but when I got there I parked, and while I was waiting, the lil bitch from the back seat of his car that first day we kicked it, she was poppin' off. "Bitch you still pulling up, like bye, go away." I just ignored her ass at first. "Get out the car and hit the blade bitch, since you wanna fuck with my nigga." I laughed so damn hard. "Baby I'ma boss, please don't worry about me."

"Bitch you're lame, you wanna be a pimp's girlfriend and that will never fly." K.C. was pulling up, he watched the bitch from a distance. "What the fuck you doing? Why you standing around looking stupid?" He asked her as he hopped out of the car. "Sid you good?" He asked me. "Yes, of course." Jumping in my passenger seat, he began to explain. "I'm not sure what just happened, but my bad, I'ma handle it. How's your day going though?" "It's going pretty good, I was just chilling, what about you?" We made small talk before he actually told me the news. "I fuck with you and I didn't want to be all in your business, but you let me know how you feeling, so I did what I could to help." "Ok... well, what's up? Tell me." He smiled and I smiled back. "I found your dad for you, love." "Whose dad? Not my dad?" "Yes Your dad, his name is Daniel, he go by D.T, right?" He could tell I was stuck and just handed me a folded-up piece of paper. "Here Sid, go figure that shit out and hit me whenever."

He hopped out the car to leave and I jumped out behind him. "Wait baby, wait... you did this for me? Thank you so much, I'ma hit you ... thank you." He smiled so hard. We both pulled off and went our separate ways. I arrived back to my hotel and just sat there in my car. I had parked for about 10 minutes just staring at the folded paper K.C. had given me. Took a deep breath in and opened it up. The paper said, "D.T a pimp from Oakland facing 15 to life" with his jail info and a cell number. I dialed the number quick with high expectations. "What's up, who's this?" It was an unfamiliar voice but it settled me. "I'm looking for D.T, is that you?" Could it be my dad? "Yea this me, who this?" I hung up the phone, wow, what a coward I was. What if he didn't want me as his daughter? I couldn't see no logical reason why I didn't know him unless he gave up on me. A few days later I woke up to a text that read, "Sydni? Is this you?" It was my dad. He could feel it just like I could, but what do I say to a man I haven't seen in ten years? "Yes it's me." "My baby girl, wow, how are you?" We began to text, and he let me know that this is his cell phone. "You have a phone in jail?" "Yea, you can buy one from the guards or other inmates ... I think about you and D.J every day." "Dad, why did you leave us, how did you get in jail?" I asked him a million questions. He said he would tell me all about it if I promise to come see him just once. "I promise." I went back home a few days later, and there Sasha meet me at the airport. "Baby I missed you, please tell me you're ok?" "Hey Sash, yea I'm good, did a little soul searching." She smiled and hugged me so tight, I knew she would understand. I needed to tell her about K, my dad, and everything, but I knew it had to be at the right time. "Well, the girls are all home waiting for us, we have a big surprise for you." "A surprise for me?" I giggled a little. "Aww you guys didn't have to! So, what is it Sash? Tell me." I tried tickling it out of her. "Nope; hop in the car and let's go."

We parked and got out the car but before we went in, Sash stopped me at the door and said, "Ok babe, go upstairs, shower and get dressed. I bought you something fly to put on, and text me when you ready to come down." I was smiling so hard thinking 'bout how much these bitches loved me. When we went inside, I saw no one from the entrance view so I just ran right up to my room and did as told. I wanted to call my dad and just say hi, but I was nervous, I called K.C instead. He didn't answer. I slipped into the shower, washed my hair and just closed my eyes thinking about the way he touched me. I needed that, I wanted some more of that.

When I got out the shower, there was his text ... "What's up baby? I'm in LA right now handling some business, can I call you when I'm done?" LA? OMG, yes he's here; this was so perfect. "Yes, that's fine, just hit me. I'm in LA too." I don't recall telling him I lived here but he did mention he looked me up or did his homework on me, so maybe he knows. I was keeping secrets from everyone; I didn't want a life of lies. I wasn't lying though either, I just would say less.

I headed downstairs and the living room was dim, I stepped to hit the light switch and outta nowhere, all these people jumped up yelling, "Surprise!" "Happy Birthday Sid!" "What? No way!" I looked down at my phone to check the date and a text came in from my dad. "Happy 18th birthday beautiful. I never left you, I'm still here." It was him, my dad did this because no one else knew. I covered my face with my hand trying to hide my tears. "Oh my God you guys, thank you." I went to hug everyone in the crowd and saw Mesh. "Look at my birthday gurl, I'm so proud of you!" I started balling in tears, she just held me tight. "I always got you sis, I promise." "Turn around Sid. Somebody else wants to wish you happy birthday." I shook my head. I was nervous and overwhelmed but Mesh did it for me, she spun me around by my shoulders and D.J popped a water balloon in my face. I stood there soaked but Mesh tossed me a water gun and we chased him through the house. He finally slipped and fell behind the island in the kitchen, that's where we got his ass. He got up to hug me. "I'm sorry, but today ain't about me, happy birthday ugly." "Thank you, I'm so glad you're here."

My brother is all I have left in this world, an extension of my mom. I was enjoying every part of my day, but where was Sash hiding at. "Hey, Mia where's Sash?" "I'm not sure baby, look outside." I was about to call her until she stood up holding a golden number 18 balloon. She felt me, she always did.

I made my way to her grabbing snacks as they came by on a platter, but I could see two glasses of champagne and a guy in the water with Sasha. What the hell was she doing? I know this bitch ain't bring a nigga to my shit. I got worked up so quick but then I thought maybe the dude came with D and it's Sasha, my bitch, I can trust her. "Hey baby, who you over here with? What you doing, I was looking for you?" She smiled and said, "Are you having a bomb ass day baby? You look so happy!" "Yea it's pretty dope." I was talking to her out loud but pointing quietly asking, "Who the fuck is this?" "But yea come here, let's go sit down and talk somewhere," she replied. "No babe, get in let's all talk right here, we were waiting for you."

The nigga who I thought was weird and wouldn't turn around to look at me was my nigga, it was K.C "Happy birthday Sid, I don't mean to come off as a creep, but you was taking too long to let me in, so I let myself in." Damn, I was so attracted to this man. "Sasha how you feeling?" "I like him mommy, this a go," she said nodding her head, and biting her lips. We all started dying laughing. K.C. picked me up and gently put me in the water in front of him. "Sash, go grab another bottle for us," he said pulling me in closer. He was an alpha male I could tell by the way he naturally demanded his position within my life. "Come here baby, I know you dying to give me that lil shit." "Dying ha, not dying though." I was laughing so hard, pussy throbbing, literally dying to give it to him, he was right. "Yea nigga, dying to give me that shit, you can give it here today though." "Oh is that so, why today?" "You bad and all, but I can't be out here fucking no 17-year-old." "You goofy." We both started laughing. "I feel it though, plus you ain't know you was dealing with a boss." "Naw I knew that, otherwise I woulda never wasted my time baby."

Sash came back with the bottle. "Sash, pour that shit, baby girl," he said. She poured us all a glass and everyone else made their way outside to join us. My brother and K greeted each other with a handshake and a nod, you know how niggas do. They already knew each other apparently, and that was cool with me. D.J raised his glass up and said, "To my baby sister, I'm proud of you nigga, and happy 18th birthday to a true boss." "D.J is her brother?" Lilly whispered to Mia. I pointed my finger at her. "Aye, you better keep yo eyes over here bitch," everybody started laughing because my bro was known for snatching niggas snow. "Yea that's my big headed brother ... thank you bro, I love you. Again, I'm so glad you're here." "Cheers!" All the glasses clinked together, and the music came on the outside speakers surrounding the pool area, my party was perfect.

D.J and Mesh brung out my cake "happy birthday to you, happy birthday to you, happy birthday dear Sydni, happy birthday to you." "Aye one of y'all cut this cake, sis we finna head out. Pull up on me tomorrow when you get up." "Ok for sure, bye Mesh." They left, and my girls went wild. I wanted them to enjoy the night, but I was ready to get this one on one with K.C. I'm sure he had plenty threesomes, but I wasn't on that. "I wanna shower this pool water off then can we chill, just you and I" "Yea that's exactly how I'm feeling, come in, I'll grab some towels."

I took him to my room and showed him my bathroom area. "Shower and you can put your bag in my closet, meet me downstairs when you done, k?" "Yup right on, see you in a second." I didn't want to come off too strong or too ready, so I left him to be alone. I wasn't a virgin, but I had only fucked one guy, a hand full of times, so I knew how to take things slow. K.C met me downstairs after his shower, and we went for a walk. "I'm feeling you but we gotta be on the same page," he said. "I agree, and I'm not trying to waste your time or mines but as you can see, I've been pretty independent for some time now." I replied. He smiled and we made plans for me to come by his house next week and check out his program. "No pressure, I just want you to be sure." "Oh, but I am sure." I knew I wanted to pursue him, I just didn't know how. "Well if you're sure, then what are we doing down here taking a walk?" We both laughed "My bad I'm just ... it's new for me that's all." He grabbed my hand and took me back inside. "You 18, right?" "Yes, why?" K.C was grinning so hard, that's when he lifted me up, grabbed a bottle of rose off the kitchen counter and headed up stairs. He was skipping steps, I knew he was strong but now I could see it. He kissed me so soft from my lips to my lips, and on the way down he got more aggressive and deeper. "Let me take care of you, I got us." It's always hard to tell if a nigga likes you for you, or for what he could get out of you. I wasn't thinking about this in the moment because all I could fix my mind on was his teeth nibbling at my pussy. "Ok baby, take care of me, take care of us." We fucked for the first time and we also made a big ass mess. "Why you ain't tell me you was a squirter?" he asked "I didn't even know, honestly." I was embarrassed as hell. I had never experienced dick like that. "It's all good, that shit go crazy, you like 1 out of 5 you know that, right?" "What you mean?" He was trying to tell me the ratio of girls being squirters and apparently, I was rare. "I'm saying umm, yo pussy good baby." "Ok, say that then." We laid there cuddling until the sun came up and I watched him go to sleep. He looked so innocent, and peaceful while asleep, but when woke, he looked dangerous. I liked the fact that he had his own money and was well connected. I liked how he took so much interest in me that he got up in my business a little. I couldn't wait to get in his and move forward. The next day was Sunday, I had been calling up to the jail trying to get onto the list to visit my dad, and I finally got a visit for Monday. I didn't mention it to my dad, I really wanted to just surprise him. "Thompson, let's go, you got a visit." I could hear him coming, walking past every visit room looking to see people. My dad had been locked up for 10 years now; I had so many things to ask him. "Sidney? Is it really you?" He couldn't believe it "Yes it's me, how are you?" We had an hour to visit with each other, but it felt like it was only 20 minutes. I wasn't ready for the things my dad was about to tell me. "I killed the man who killed your mom, that's why I'm here." I knew my dad was a pimp, but I didn't know he was a killer also. "Damn dad, what part of the game is that?" "I don't know Sid, I tried to get out but... but .... I don't know, just did what I had to do." The politics to this game will get hectic, yes, I knew this, but my dad was facing life behind a bitch. I had to help him somehow, this shit just didn't sit well with me.

Tamba Beasley

Free My Pops.

Chapter 10

The Outcome

After visiting with my pops, I asked K.C to refer me some lawyers and told him what my plans were. He was with it and said he'd do whatever he could to help me out. I was now wondering if D.J knew what was up with our dad. He never talked about him or told me anything like this, maybe he didn't know. I had to find out so I called him up and asked. "D.J, what you up to?" Before we fell out we would always check in. "Who this, Sid?" "Yea it's me. My bad I haven't pulled up on you, I got busy with some stuff." "It's all good. I'm just chilling, what you on?" He sounded like he was in bed still so I got straight to it. "Ok, so, I found dad." "What you mean found him? Where he at?" "So, you really don't know nothing?" I was trying to find a way to test him, but he seemed sincere. "Last I knew, dad moved to Miami and started a new family on us." "Dad is in jail; he killed the man who killed our mom." The phone got silent and I knew that feeling of finally knowing something. It was the beginning of something for us, all these years we thought nobody on this earth loved us enough to just stick around. Shit, everybody left us, they died and or they just left.

"What you mean Sid? How do you know this?" He asked. "Because I found him somehow. Long story short, I went to visit him and he told me." "How do you know it's him?" "It's him I'm certain bro." I knew he felt reassured after I confirmed but we sat quietly on the phone consumed in our own thoughts. "I want you to come with me on the next visit in two days." I didn't know what to expect at this point, but I knew I had to try. Never give up on family, my mom always told me that, so I was fighting hard and never giving up on what was left. The next day I had a long list of things planned with Sasha. It was hard tying to divide my time equally between my brother, my dad, my nigga, my bitch, and my business, I could just die. You would think there were two or three me's running around. Anyway, Sasha had us in DTLA running errands when we ran right into K.C. "What's up with blood?" He said to us jokingly, I needed that type of energy. Everything was serious and intense for me, I wanted to laugh and not think for a second. I laughed out loud, trying to laugh extra hard. Sasha gave me a look that could kill, she wasn't gon keep quiet either. "You laughing real hard though." "Yes I am, and your point is?" I was ready to tear her to pieces about my peace. "Sash chill I'm just laughing, I think I deserve a little laughter, don't you?" She nodded yes because nothing else made sense, either she was my bitch and on what I'm on, or she could catch her cut, and she knew that. "Babe can it be just us today?" Sasha asked. I knew she wanted alone time but damn, what more could we possibly do? I had already spent the entire morning and afternoon with just her. "It's whatever," was my reply. "K.C, I'll link up with you a little later k, we gotta finish up a few things." "Bet" he kissed my forehead and waved goodbye to Sasha. "So, what's next boo?" I asked looking off into the distance, wondering which way to go now. "I made us reservations, this way babe." Now it was all starting to make sense why Sasha was acting weird, she just wanted to follow through on her plans, and I felt that. We arrived at a chic little lunch spot and sunk our bodies into their couches. Each table had a couch to lounge and relax, so we did. I thought things were perfect until it happened, I got that one phone call nobody ever wants to get. "Sid where are you? D.J just got shot up in Oakland; I'm following the ambulance to the hospital!" Mesh was yelling at me to hurry and meet her. "What the fuck! Nooo! When how? I just talked to him... I'm in LA, what happened?" "I don't know, I don't know. Just get here please, I don't want him to die. Lord why him?" "Ok I'm coming mesh please don't let him die, I'm finna hop on the road. I love you sis, stay strong. He's gon make it." I was still in a daze at the news. "What? What happened! Hello Sidney!!" "D.J got shot, let's go." I picked back up my phone to call someone. "Dad they shot up D.J, he's headed to the hospital." I barely fucking knew this man, how I sound calling him dad, but it felt so natural. "I heard baby girl, but don't go to the hospital yet." "But why not? I need to be there with him." "Trust me on this. They not done with him, get somewhere safe baby. I love you." "I don't know who to trust dad, tell me what to do, please." I begged him ... "Call K.C, tell him what happened, you can trust him." "What the fuck!" "What Sid, what's wrong?" "Nothing, he hung up. Pull over please." I had scatter brain thinking about my brother, but even more from thinking how my dad and K.C were connected. I got out the car to call Mesh. I called her and called her back to back, no answer. "Aye dial Mesh from your phone for me, she not answering." I didn't know what the fuck was going on, but shit just wasn't right. I called K.C's number and got him on the phone. I was crying and talking so fast, "Baby slow down, where are you? It's gon be ok. Just send me yo location, I'm coming." I couldn't figure this shit out and I was scared too, I hope my brother is ok. "Did Mesh answer?" I asked Sasha ... "no babe, no answer" that's when K.C. pulled up and bounced out his car "Aye, we gotta get up out of here ASAP, park your car over there let's go! Hurry up!" What the fuck was happening? I grabbed all my shit out the car and hopped in his driver seat. "Sasha hurry." She ran over to the car, and another car was speeding up the way, headed in our direction. We pulled off slowly with the lights off and turned down the next street waiting until the car passed. In a matter of minutes, gun shots rung through the area while someone shot up my car and quickly sped off. "Can you tell me what's going on K, because I'm scared, I really am?" He held me tight. We hit the road and started driving towards Vegas. "Damn, they was gon kill you too." "What do you mean too? Is D.J dead?" "No, my bad. I mean, I don't know, but they killed his girl." "What girl? Was he with a girl when he got shot or is it Mesh? You remember Mesh, was it her?" "I don't know, Sid I just got the call after we hung. My boy said D.J's girl got lit up getting off the freeway." I just went numb, but nothing was confirmed. When we finally made it to Vegas five hours later, we pulled up to a house, I didn't want to ask hella questions in front of Sasha so I waited. "Sasha, this my spot. You can go inside and make yourself at home. I need to holler at Sidney real quick." "Ok papa." She smiled at me for reassurance and once she was gone, I turned to K.C and thanked him. He knew exactly what to do and he really got my back. "You gon be ok here for as long as you need to be, but I gotta get back to my business." "Wait, are you leaving right now?" I asked. "I gotta catch a flight to Atlanta baby, you know this shit don't stop." He was right; I wouldn't be fair if I begged him to stay. "I'll be back as soon as I'm done." "Alright, I mean I don't even know what to say, text me when you make it?" "Of course, aye, and relax, everything is going to be fine." He said that like it was a true statement, but I didn't feel him. "Ok baby, see you soon." And just like that, he was gone again. I went inside to Sasha playing some music videos on the main room's T.V. "Baby, let's get in the pool; it's so nice out here." Ava was blowing up both me and Sasha's phone. I wasn't ready to deal with my girls yet, so I made a plan. "In the morning, you call the girls, tell them what happened with D.J and that I'm dealing with it, and I'll make arrangements to get them." "Ok" "and tell them to stay on those programs too?" "Yes, definitely." I needed to hear from my brother, so I called the hospital a million times, but I couldn't get through. Around 3 p.m. the next day, K.C. called me from a private number. "You good?" "Yes, I'm good, but I can't get through to the hospital. They've got code names and all these safety precautions to follow, how am I supposed to know what's up?" He just listened for a minute ... "oh shit, have Lilly go down there, she can scope it out. Tell her to see who's in the waiting room and to find out if he's ok." "Right, ok. I don't know why I didn't think of that, call me later, k?" "Later." I called Lily and she went to highland hospital right away. I started to feel better and hopeful, like good news was going to come from this. I felt like I had abandoned my fucking brother I felt like a sucka, like I been running the opposite way from where he was. I felt like he needed me, but I wasn't even there, but what could I do having pulled up five hours later? I shoulda gone, I should be there; I should be there. I played the blame game for a few hours waiting on Lilly to give me something. "Bitch, what is taking you so damn long? Tell me something!" "Babe, calm down. I been asking and waiting. They keep saying they would let me know soon." "Ughhhhhhhhhh!" I yelled as loud as I could. "Ok, soon as you know something call me." I hung up, pacing the floors of this fucking house like a lunatic. What the fuck did D.J do?

When you fonking in these streets, you gotta have your money up and that's just period, a general rule to go by. You gotta be smart and know that the type of niggas you playing with will either pull the trigger because it's cool and they lame as fuck, or because the price is right. I knew plenty of guys who could easily put some money on a nigga head My brother is a different type of nigga though, he gonna pull the trigger because he has nothing else to live for.

About the Author

About the Author

Tamba Beasley was born in Los Angeles raised in Oakland California she is 31 years old and has two daughters ages 11 and 3. She currently resides in Las Vegas Nevada with her children and fiancé

Tamba is truly an Oakland native who grew the love of writing at a very young age while being a boys and girls club member she was first presented an opportunity into a writing contest and did pretty good. later on while attending community day school she was entered into a state mystery writing contest and won. She then fell in love and has been known for her mystery short novels and poetry every since. With dreams of becoming an author, here's her first novel She belongs to the game part 1.